LIES AND LOVE IN ALASKA

Marsh Rose

Coastal Arts Publishing
Cloverdale, CA

LIES AND LOVE IN ALASKA

Copyright 2013 Marsh Rose
All rights reserved

Coastal Arts Publishing
P.O. Box 907
Cloverdale, CA   95425

No part of this book may be reproduced without written permission, except for brief quotations to books and critical reviews. This story is a work of fiction. Characters and events are a product of the author's imagination. Any resemblance to individuals, living or dead, is coincidental.

ISBN 978-0-9856205-1-6

Book Design by Kathryn Marcellino
Photograph by Hal Brindlay

Printed in the United States

Acknowledgments

Writing occurs in solitude but it takes a village to publish the result. The author is indebted to Carol Costello for generous time and guidance, Adair Lara for decades of mentoring, Kathryn Marcellino, Diane Bartleson, Donna Casey and Hal Brindley.

—Marsh Rose
amon101@att.net

"There's a land—oh, it beckons and beckons,
and I want to go back—and I will."

– Robert Service
The Spell Of The Yukon, 1906

PART ONE:

CALIFORNIA, 1989

Chapter 1

The Odds Are Good

It was the day after Christmas. Annalee Perkins leaned on her counter and listened to the rain pinging into a galvanized bucket in the next aisle. She dreaded the coming hours. Only Valentine's Day was as demoralizing as the holiday season at Home And Garden Land. Around her, fellow H.A.G.L. workers drifted in, hung their sodden rain gear and began to prepare for the long day ahead.

The intercom roared to life. Feedback sliced along the cinder block walls, then Annalee heard the voice of her boss Marvin. "Stupefied," he thundered. "Five letters, sixty-three down, third letter Z." Marvin began each day with the morning paper's crossword and he seldom finished it alone. There was a moment of silence, then a reply boomed from the bookkeeper's microphone.

"Dazed."

Annalee sighed. Her knees ached and she felt older than her 40 years. Reluctantly she shifted her gaze to the window. Outside in the rain, ten women had formed a line at the door. Their clothing, from muddy blue jeans to elegant pants suits, represented the wide range of incomes in the rural northern California wine country. But their faces wore nearly identical expressions of dismay. Each woman carried an object—a bathroom scale, a hose attachment or a set of crescent wrenches, some with festive wrapping paper still attached. When H.A.G.L.'s hangar-like doors opened, they would stride to Annalee's counter and imply that she, maven of the complaints department, was somehow to blame because their husbands or lovers had shopped for Christmas gifts at the hardware store when they should have been at the jeweler's. Then Annalee would spend the day issuing return receipts, doling out refunds, pleading for stock boys and occasionally reassuring a crestfallen customer that the customer was indeed worth more, so much more than this offensive dashboard cover and matching automotive cup holder and trash receptacle.

"Men," Annalee thought. "They can not accomplish even the most simple requirement of love. A gift." She congratulated herself. Never again would she find a brightly-wrapped garbage disposal brush under the tree. And while she would pass Valentine's Day alone, she would not open another box with a bow to find a selection of AA, AAA and D batteries.

She reached for a shop broom and turned to her immediate chore, sweeping up the evidence of mice. H.A.G.L. was damp and drafty to the loyal but long-suffering staff, but for all other species its accommodations were a luxury relative to wintering in the muddy field outside. So with the freezing December rains came a parade of insects, amphibians, birds, bats and rodents to join the swarms of customers.

Someone called her name. She looked up to see her friend Ivy, The Duchess Of Kitchenware, with her faux tiara anchored in her hair by a rubber band under her chin. "Got something for you," she called. "Meet me in the staff lounge for lunch." She waved what appeared to be a magazine. Knowing Ivy, it would be something in the realm of dating, being single, or women her age finding love. Or at least sex.

Annalee sighed again.

―

In the H.A.G.L. staff lounge Annalee and Ivy unpacked their lunches. Tuna sandwich and tea for Annalee, Diet Pepsi in Ivy's lunch cooler along with a jumbo package of potato chips.

"Have some chips," Ivy offered. "You know, it's too bad they didn't leave the showers when H.A.G.L. took over the building from Greyhound." She gestured at the wall where shower stall dividers had stood. "If the bus drivers could clean up in here, why couldn't we? Hose a layer of that H.A.G.L. dust down the drain and be dewy fresh for the afternoon rush. Should there ever be an afternoon rush."

"Showers would be good as long as we don't get our hair wet. I think Marvin bought that last lot of hair dryers from gnomes on an island where they don't have electricity. Anyway, let's get it over with. What's this important article you brought for me?"

Ivy fished in her purse and withdrew the slick publication she had brandished that morning. "It's not just an article, Annalee. It's a whole magazine. I think you'll like it."

"And that's why your eyes are squeezed up like when you're talking about your next round of gum surgery. Hand it over."

Annalee took the magazine and glanced at its cover. She saw an auburn-haired man smiling into the distance. He wore a red ski parka with its hood encircled by a ruff of white fur trim and his arms were around the neck of a white dog with strange blue eyes. Behind them was a sled and in the background a white mountain range. Annalee fanned the pages. She saw nothing but photographs of individual men over sparse paragraphs of print. Puzzled, she returned to the cover and then laughed. "*Alaskan Bachelors*! What is this, a mail order groom catalogue for Eskimos?"

"Nothing like that," her friend said soberly. "It's the biggest thing in the singles scene, way better than personal ads in the paper. It's on all the talk shows and in all the bookstores, Annalee. All the men in there are single. They live in Alaska where there aren't any women, or hardly any, and you can meet them through the magazine. And it's perfectly safe. The people in the magazine interview them to make sure they're not weird."

"You've been reading this yourself, haven't you? I can just hear Mike. 'Sure, Ivy, what the hell. We've been married long enough, good a time as any to bring some fresh blood into the scene. I'll just mosey on down to the bus depot and pick up our Alaskan bachelor and his sled dogs while you put the moose in the oven.' Oh, look, someone's been kissing this picture. I see lipstick and it's your shade!"

"Annalee, come on. It's been five years. Your husband and that slut he ran off with have had two kids already and you're still hiding from relationships. Everything you wear is black or brown. No makeup, no accessories, no jewelry other than your wedding rings that look like a row of klieg lights. You're like a Civil War widow. Do you know what some people call you?"

Annalee grimaced. "'The Widder Perkins.'"

"Right. So take off the goddamned rings, put on a red dress and let a nice man get close to you. It's bad enough you moved back to your childhood home when Brad dumped you. Leave the past. Go forward, Annalee. It's 1990 next week, a whole new decade!"

"Ivy, please. You know my parents need me to watch the house while they're away, and the singles scene for women my age is just foolishness, fantasy and sometimes danger. Do you know of any available man our age who isn't alcoholic, crazy or secretly married?" Annalee reached for the pepper mill and vigorously ground it over her sandwich. "Here in San Amaro a new lover's moves in bed would be common knowledge because his most recent ex would have confided to the checkout clerk at Vera's Market. And outside the circled wagons of San Amaro? It's not just a jungle out there. It's another planet. Remember Marilyn's so-called boyfriend Geoffrey?"

"That was an exception, Annalee."

"Marilyn finding out two weeks after they got together that Geoffrey was born Gloria and had placed third in the women's open golf tournament at Chula Vista? Not all that exceptional, Ivy. And Lorene's boyfriend from Los Angeles?"

"Get out! He used to be a woman?"

"No, but she told me he asked to wear the peach lace thongs he'd spied in her underwear drawer. And what about Francine? Gives up six generations of Roman Catholicism, joins a singles vision quest and all she gets is hepatitis from drinking bad river water."

"You're just focusing on the negative. And besides, all those women were losers. Look at you, with those long legs and red hair. You can get any man you want."

"Thanks but even if it were true there's too much technology. Everywhere you look it's breast implants, lip plumping, thigh reduction. I don't need the competition. The whole thing just leads to misery. There's no one out there for me. I mean, what are the odds of me finding a good man?"

"The odds are good, Annalee. But you'll never know if you don't try." Ivy met her friend's eyes and held them while she reached down to slide *Alaskan Bachelors* closer to Annalee's side of the table.

Annalee rolled her eyes and shoved the magazine into her purse. "Let's get back to work, Ivy. There are blenders to blend, gaskets to gask and H.A.G.L. workers to sell them."

That night Annalee gazed at her bedroom ceiling in the dark. A quarter moon had plied its course across her window and now only its silver light cast a dim glow in the room where she had slept as a teenager—sometimes waking with thoughts similar to those she now tried to still. Relationships. Long ago it was her desire for romance and now it was her desire to avoid it but many of its chores and puzzles were oddly similar. What to give up, what to withhold.

Ivy and her schemes. The most recent wasn't the worst but it was bad enough. She had convinced an old classmate to come from San Diego under the pretext of attending their high school reunion. "Just let me introduce you to Henry, Annalee," Ivy had pleaded. "He could play any musical instrument in the high school band just by looking at it. 'Henry The Great,' the band leader used to call him."

Henry The Great had whined about Ivy's cooking, barely glanced at Annalee, and left two days early. Annalee alone was pleased with his early departure. Possibly some internal medical problem, she theorized. He seemed sanitary enough but his fishy-smelling breath could stop traffic. And Ivy's third cousin Barry, the engineer from Seattle. Annalee finally conceded to a phone conversation. On the predetermined night, Barry phoned and spent an hour alternately vilifying and glorifying his ex-wife. And Annalee couldn't imagine being intimate with a man whose hobby was exotic snakes. His description of his atrium with its climate-controlled haven for pit vipers made her imagine something cold slithering up her leg. There were too many women her age out there competing for men, left single by the devastation and permission of the 1960s and 1970s. No relationships forged in her generation seemed to last, and she was disheartened by the pathos of personal ads, singles bars, and her persistent matrimonial agents.

Annalee shifted again in bed. Her shoulders were suddenly chill and she pulled the covers higher. For five years her mother and Ivy and their friends had initiated a parade through her life of single, middle-aged sons, nephews, cousins, neighbors, all divorced and desperate, or gay and in the closet, or separated and angry, or not available because of another woman or a secret vice or in one case a 50 year old man who had never had a girlfriend, lived in his parents' basement and collected teddy bears. And that ridiculous "male-order" magazine from Alaska, now bundled up with the discarded newspapers and circulars in the recycling bin in the garage.

Annalee's thoughts rolled to a halt and she drummed her fingers on the sheets. What if, she thought, she could stop this incessant meddling in her life with one well-placed demonstration of its futility. Just a harmless prank. Those men in Alaska...they were all desperate up there. Surely one would respond to an overture from a middle-aged hardware store employee. She could write to one of those men. Lying there in the dark, Annalee played with the idea. She would never have to meet him in person, just leak the intrigue to her social world. Her long-distance liaison would temporarily be all things to people who loved her. Her parents would believe she had found someone. Ivy would be thrilled to hear his fascinating letters read aloud in the staff lunchroom, the drama of the Last Frontier, bears, violent weather, long eerie nights. The town would cease gossiping about her pathetic solitude. And soon, the denouement. Perhaps with help from a discreet private investigator, her Alaskan bachelor would be exposed as married, psychotic, addicted to alcohol or heroin or sex, emotionally married to his mother, a felon hiding from the law, a deadbeat father hiding from his kids, and/or simply too antisocial to be relationship material. All middle aged men who were out trolling for single women were like that. At their age why else would they be seeking love? Or at least sex. Then her matchmakers would agree that Baby Boomer dating was unrealistic. Ivy would apologize for nagging. Her mother would accept her as she was. The town would leave her alone. She would be vindicated.

But no. Annalee sighed and turned over to sleep. Even for a harmless prank the idea was risky. Annalee no longer took risks.

Chapter 2

The Princess of Complaints

In her ten years of employment Annalee had watched Home And Garden Land become the lifeblood of the newly lucrative wine, agriculture and ranching industries in the sprawling rural area an hour north of the Golden Gate Bridge. She took pride in its role in her community. On its shelves vintners could find the irrigation supplies that nurtured their Pinot Noir, a fruit so delicate and temperamental that it earned its name, "the heartbreak grape." Sheep ranchers came to H.A.G.L. for shears, dairy farmers bought rubber teats for their milking machines, and apple and prune growers found the rare three-legged ladders specific to their harvests. Even the wealthy transplants from Los Angeles, starry-eyed with unrealistic dreams, could find the fencing supplies they needed to corral the unfortunate llamas and ostriches they imported from climates far different than that of coastal northern California.

Annalee didn't mind that her place of employment was also unwittingly a source of local entertainment and sometimes hilarity. Other than the post-Christmas and Valentine shopping fiascos when she would end the day with tears of exhaustion, lately she enjoyed the work spirit. H.A.G.L.'s former owners, twin brothers Hector and Hugo Phee, had shown no concern for staff morale. Turnover had been high and there had been formal complaints to California Occupational Safety and Health Association about the drafty corners and leaking tin roof. Eight years ago the twins retired and turned the reins over to Hector's son Marvin. Shy and socially awkward, Marvin determined to reverse the dark ambience and under his supervision Home and Garden Land was now a tiny universe. Small appliances were organized around an island where the cash register was housed in a thatched hut. In a faux port an actual ship's mast rose almost to the ceiling above plumbing supplies. Stuffed parrots and monkeys in a make-believe jungle looked down at customers who shopped for gardening supplies, and refrigerators were lined up in a row and dressed as Easter Island megaliths. Of course viticulture supplies were sold from a fabricated winery which featured an authentic stone entryway and oak barrels. In real wineries the barrels rumble and echo with the sound of fermentation. At H.A.G.L. those same sounds were broadcast over the loudspeaker at half-hour intervals.

At Marvin's behest each employee wore a crown and a badge with an honorary title, including elderly security guard Cyrus, The Knight Of Twilight. The staff occasionally took a dim view of Marvin's more baroque eccentricities. At the last staff meeting there had been murmurs of mutiny when Marvin, with his eyes moist and gleaming, suggested thrones at each cash register and one for T'Angeline Duffy, The Lady Of The Forklift. But most of the workers were secretly proud of their whimsical store.

Annalee liked her boss Marvin, and he in turn adored Annalee, The Princess Of Complaints, for the comforting femininity she projected amid the stock boxes, oily rags and dust at her Island Of All Returns. While few customers came to the complaints department unless they were unhappy, the interaction with Annalee was seldom acrimonious. "Now, let's have a look at the problem," she would suggest as she accepted a copper valve with a handle that, according to its stony-faced owner, had been welded shut in the factory, probably in some act of Union defiance. She would place it on her counter as if it were a sick puppy and attempt to twist the handle. "Oh, that is impossible, isn't it?" she would murmur. Then she would place drops of machine oil on the fixture. "The manufacturers tighten it so that it doesn't rattle loose in transit," she might say, including the customer in her occult knowledge while she covertly allowed a moment for the oil to penetrate. Then she would reach for her pliers and gently work the fitting loose, careful never to imply that her experience and patience, much less the tensile strength in her slender wrists, might be superior to those of the customer. Charmed by Annalee's serenity, her red hair under her crown and her tinkling bracelets, the shopper would leave soothed and smiling.

Annalee liked the customers, many of whom she had known since her teens when her family moved to San Amaro. She respected the women, so determined to be independent, frowning over their lists of washers and gaskets. And the men. She appreciated the way they trolled the aisles in their work boots and paint-spattered overalls, smelling of oil and earth, sweat and aftershave. She liked their shaggy hair, their solemn expressions and the way they spoke so softly. But although she liked them, she had no desire to feel one of those calloused hands caress her body or to press her lips to a bearded cheek.

Her lack of desire for men wasn't acrimonious or bitter. No one would witness Annalee at a support group, proclaiming a history of abuse at their hands. In fact, Annalee came from a family where love was easy, accessible, and anticipated. She had enjoyed the teenage thrills and angst of sexual maturity, then a passionate romance followed by traditional marriage. That had been her life for 35 years.

And then there was one clean division, bright and sharp as a scalpel. When she now thought of love before that moment, it was as if through a pane of jewel-toned glass ... colorful but untouchable. Since that day there was her life after love.

She grew up in San Francisco. By age 14 she was taller than most girls in her class and the long limbs and red hair she had despised as a child were now looks favored by young models in *Vogue*. She realized that certain boys, those with odd elements of distance and intensity, could cause feelings she instinctively knew not to discuss with her parents. She noticed that they watched her, as did her young history teacher whom she caught gazing at her behind when she turned back to ask a question. When she was allowed to date at 16 she chose carefully. Each young man who drew her attention had in common some nucleus of obsession. Music, math, sculpture, theater, his specific passion didn't matter as long as his total commitment to Annalee remained just out of her reach. Sexual maturity came into full flower in her junior year in high school where the rich mix was drawn from every corner of the San Francisco metropolis. She lost her virginity to a talented African pianist who had come to the city from Kenya on a music scholarship.

Annalee enjoyed the flow and texture of each fascination. She craved the glimpse into each untested world that could be offered in a new relationship with such a boy. While she had no interest in the theater, she liked to be taken to dress rehearsals with Alec and to sit in the darkened second row and absorb from a distance the electric energy of the stage. At the racetrack she watched from the sidelines as her current boyfriend Monty obeyed the demands of the pit crew and fueled a Lamborghini with frantic haste or rolled a spent tire away, dodging the young men with replacements as they rushed forward. She attracted the attention of a brilliant young computer aficionado from her father's office. Their only kiss was on the roof of the building under stars that were dimmed from the reflected neon lights of Mission Street below.

And then in November of 1970, a change. Annalee's father, Cooper Michaels, son of Donato and Albertine Molise, ended his career as an architect for a corporate engineering firm in San Francisco and moved his family—wife Rachel and daughters Annalee and Evelyn—100 miles north to the wine country. On the outskirts of rural San Amaro he formed Michaels Viticulture and began to design the filters, tanks, irrigation controls and presses for the burgeoning wine industry. Within a year, this first-generation son of Italian immigrants had become a living legend among the vintners of San Amaro. If he was sometimes too aggressive and voluble, his Type A personality drove him to excellence and he was soon the only resource they would use to expand and maintain the wineries their fathers and, in some cases, grandfathers had established when they too came over from Italy and saw those rolling hills and liquid golden sunshine so much like Tuscany.

Annalee's mother and her younger sister Evelyn adjusted to rural life, albeit in different ways.

Rachel glided through the required status shift in tandem with her husband and returned to San Francisco on regular shopping forays to the pricey salons. She favored sleek monochromatic tunics with pressed slacks, understated silver jewelry and an elegant platinum coiffeur that accentuated her high cheekbones.

Evelyn, then a high school freshman, arrived in San Amaro poised to take the country boys by storm. Her packing boxes brimmed with garments from North Beach consignment shops. She wore gauze and leather, carefully crafted tatters and fringes. While she had been just another offbeat high school girl in San Francisco, she stunned the San Amaro adolescent community with her beads, spider web-like shawls and worn blue jeans. She had developed a husky rasp and had perfected the sidelong gaze that would become her hallmark. She emulated her idol Janis Joplin whose death the previous month was still sending shock waves through her generation.

Social adjustment was more difficult for Annalee. For her, the moving van that took the family's possessions to San Amaro might have been a rocket ship heading for distant galaxies. If the young men of San Francisco had been visits to exotic new worlds, the boys of San Amaro were island exile. They were the soulless academic types, or loud boys who drank too much, or the thick-necked football jocks. And, as with any small town that offered little diversion, there were the motorcycle boys. The Pack Rats sported tight jeans, heavy square-toed black boots with metal accessories, and black jackets with the letters PR and a malevolent rat face with red eyes embroidered on the back above a Harley-Davidson logo. They dated the tough girls whose parents worked the lumber mills and vineyards. Annalee could have snagged such a boy to quell her desire for vicarious adventure but they offered little of that reserve she craved beyond their superficial dislike of authority. Annalee suspected that their disdain melted into sniveling cooperation when they were told to toe the line. They swaggered from the principal's office with the veneer of bravado that covers tense lack of self confidence.

In the first year at San Amaro, for Annalee dates with boys were events of stultifying boredom. She accepted an offer from Vinnie, son of Mad Mogul Discount Auto, who took her to the movies and moments after the opening credits seized her around the neck and salivated on her lips, breathing asthmatically. Annalee spent the remainder of the evening in the ladies' room, staring at the ceiling after rinsing out her mouth. Tim sat across from her on a chilly faux leather banquette at Reinhart's Truck Stop and disclosed miserably that he sometimes doubted Jesus really was The Lord. With Barry, the drummer in the high school marching band, Annalee experienced fleeting desires to experiment beyond caresses in the instrument room until he revealed that he was also attracted to Chester who played the glockenspiel and he was too confused to progress either way.

In February of Annalee's senior year, into this tar pit of ennui came Bradford Perkins.

Chapter 3

Love and Confusion

The rumors flew. One held that the mysterious Bradford Perkins had been sent to San Amaro to live with his grandparents after a felony charge of mayhem in San Diego, that he had bitten the thumb of an FBI secret police detective. That he was 21 years old and had failed his senior year twice, and that he held his grandparents hostage while he commandeered their house. Rumors and those tough girls with their calf-high boots and hip-hugging Levi's dogged Bradford Perkins like twin contrails after a high-flying jet.

Annalee watched Bradford Perkins swing down from his motorcycle in the high school parking lot and she felt a refreshed surge of that desire for immersion from afar. Bradford gazed at Annalee, his expression registered nothing, and he looked away toward Sharon McKinney who leaned against the schoolyard fence, exhaling cigarette smoke through her nostrils. When Annalee saw him put his feet on his desk in algebra class she felt a tingling in her ankles. He gazed out of the window and rolled his toothpick and the observing Annalee could feel the wood against her teeth. While the Pack Rats were openly hostile to faculty and then paid for their disrespect with detention and classroom chores, Bradford addressed his teachers with a polite ma'am or sir, then dismissed them. He treated the fawning motorcycle boys with casual disinterest. It was whispered that he did not simply ride a motorcycle. He raced. As a mere adolescent, it was murmured in the halls of San Amaro High, he had broken the sound barrier on a Harley with a parachute in back.

Annalee knew that Bradford Perkins caught her staring. He must have noticed that she turned up in unlikely places. The cool redhead from a well-placed family had no business loitering outside the door to the high school metal shop. Lingering in the parking lot. Sidling past his table in the cafeteria where he sat alone. Her seeping fascination was returned with an expressionless glance.

After six weeks of tension, Bradford himself leapt the distance.

"You want a ride?"

Annalee looked up from *A Tale Of Two Cities* to meet eyes that were blue and cool as a cirque. His auburn hair shagged carelessly over his collar and forehead. He reached up to flip a cowlick out of his eye, revealing a sinewy arm and bony wrist.

"Do I want a ride where, Mister Perkins?" Her voice was level and no waver betrayed her astonished heart.

He grinned, showing a chipped front tooth. " 'Mister Perkins,' " he echoed. "Hey look. What about I trade you a ride around town for help with this Dickhead essay?"

"It's Dickens," she said. "And yes."

Annalee's first visit to the Bradford Perkins—Brad—estate two days later, to further help Brad with Charles Dickens, was instructive. Rumor did little justice to the more subtle reality. The Perkins grandparents had turned over their garage to the troubled 18 year old son of their only offspring. In return, Brad was to finish high school in San Amaro, having already failed his senior year in San Diego. If he was unsuccessful, the juvenile probation officer in Escondido, whose thumb had nearly healed, was waiting to take him back into custody. Brad reigned over his small living quarters in a way that shook Annalee to her bones. Although she had experienced vicariously the thrill of intensity in many elements, from stage to scientific laboratory, she had never seen an all-consuming focus of attention to match the obsession of Bradford Perkins.

Entering the garage she stepped around a machine so high that it towered nearly to the ceiling. It was black and bulbous, emitted a pungent oily odor and reminded her of the device that beamed constellations onto the ceiling in the planetarium in San Francisco. A long metal table was stacked with unidentifiable tools, a jar of peanut butter, coils of wire, jugs of fluid, two car batteries and a package of English muffins. With her eyes adjusting to the dim light Annalee saw, stretched along a far wall, a flat metal bed with an overhang of dials, cables and hooks.

She noticed an unmade cot on which was a thermal blanket and a stack of high school textbooks and, piled high beside it, a mélange of wheels, tires and ancient-looking hardbound manuals. The title of a fat, dusty tome on top read *Great Aircraft of History—World War II.*

"What's all this stuff?" she asked weakly.

"Machinery. It was my grandpa's and now it's mine."

"I know it's machinery. But what's it for? Are you making airplanes in here?"

Brad's laughter echoed off the walls, making a sound as if several people were chuckling at her. Then he took her hand and led her to a side room where dozens of worn books spanned racks of shelves. He opened the pages of a musty-smelling manual. "See, you take all this theory about fighter planes from World War II and you just put them inside the Harleys." He grinned over at her with his eyes alight.

Annalee was bewildered. "Put them inside the motorcycles? How?"

"Well, like, you change the fuel ratios and move the exhaust system, stuff like that." Brad closed the book and looked into the middle distance as if he had become distracted.

"Why?"

Brad did a double-take at her. "Why? So you can make the Harley go faster."

Annalee glanced around and saw no Harley-Davidson memorabilia or logos. The Pack Rats plastered those orange and black winged decals on every surface. "I don't see anything Harley in here."

"Yeah, right. Harley-Davidson stickers. Just like assholes, everybody's got to have one." Brad said the forbidden word casually as he slipped the book back into its place.

Another facet of the rumor mill fell short of reality. Brad did race his modified Harley in the rarified atmosphere of the Bonneville Salt Flats of Utah. When he was 16 he became the youngest member of the venerable Perkins racing clan to take to the track at the annual national speed trials. Brad's recent ancestry tugged at his course through life like the moon at high tide. His family's history of amateur racing extended back to 1952 and the first speed trial on the mirror-flat prehistoric lake bed at Bonneville. His grandfather and his father Alexander held land speed records and Brad dreamed of boosting the family name to new heights by adopting airplane technology to two-wheeled speed. Steeped in motorcycle lore, Brad had a lip-curling disdain for popular Harley-Davidson faddism. His comprehension of fuel, air, heat and metal was deep and intuitive. His command of the English language, written and spoken, stopped at a seventh grade level and his grasp of history was dismal. Brad believed Charlemagne was an alcoholic beverage.

Annalee had sex for the second time in her life on the rumpled cot beside the motorcycle tires and technical tomes. When she next opened her eyes it was to focus on a mildewed book titled *14,000 Gear Ratios*. For Brad it was the 18th time he'd had sexual intercourse. Or perhaps the 20th. He couldn't see keeping score, he said, exhaling unfiltered Camel smoke toward the cobwebbed ceiling while pillowing Annalee's head on his arm. He stayed friends with each girl. He'd know if one was pregnant, and none ever were.

Brad came, by late spring, to have two consuming pulls on his attention. They were his preparation for the August speed trials at Bonneville, and Annalee. If they were placed according to their value on a race track, granted, Annalee would have remained close to the starting gate. Nevertheless, her status was closer to Brad than his education, food, grandparents, friends, sleep, or anything other than the gleaming motorcycle frame on which he mounted the mechanical innards that gave the machine its life force. Those tough whiskey-voiced girls were left in the dust.

Annalee tolerated her high school graduation ceremony to please her parents, sloughed off her cap and gown in the girls' locker room, pulled on her Levi's and went to Brad's garage to stand quietly in the driveway beside the elder Mr. Perkins while Brad, his eyes narrowed with tension and concentration, started the rebuilt engine of his motorcycle for the first time that year. When his grandfather shook Brad's hand and said, "good work, kid," Annalee saw her boyfriend blush for the first time.

That he had graduated and was now out from under the mauled thumb of the juvenile probation officer was of passing interest to him. A mere seven weeks remained until the race. Brad's father Alexander was coming from San Diego with a flatbed truck for Brad and his project, which would be chained next to Alexander's own racing Harley. Then the Perkins men, grandfather too, would turn east and head for Utah.

As Brad's woman, Annalee assumed she would accompany them. She shopped for sunglasses, halter tops and other accessories appropriate for the desert in late summer. She awaited news of the time and day of their departure. Finally, swinging one leg while she sat on the scarred metal chair in Brad's garage, she asked when they might be leaving. He looked up from tightening a metal band around a length of hose, brow furrowing momentarily. Then he shook his head.

"No females allowed, Annalee. This is just how I get away from things."

She wasn't invited? Annalee was stunned. She felt the onset of outrage and disappointment. She had seen herself flinging champagne onto Brad's shirtfront while the crowd went wild and Brad accepted his trophy. "What am I," she wailed, "something you need a vacation from?"

Brad put down a wrench and looked hard into Annalee's eyes. "Annalee," he said in the tone one uses with obstinate children. "I'll see you when I get home. End of subject."

Annalee did not return to the garage for four days. When she did she wore the azure sweater that Brad said looked good with her red hair and blue eyes. She went barefoot so that Brad would feel concern for her tender feet on the grimy concrete floor. Perhaps he would carry her to the cot. Then as the sheets cooled and Brad blew cigarette smoke toward the ceiling they could discuss the trip, now two days away.

She slipped just inside the door to the garage. She could see his bare torso, white as porcelain, and the gleaming motorcycle illuminated by the blue-white blaze of a long fluorescent light hung low from a length of wire wrapped insecurely around a ceiling beam. He was bent over the chassis, holding a tiny spring in one hand. His shaggy hair was dull, sweat streamed down his naked back and his low-slung jeans appeared to have been worn since the last time she saw him. A ring of black grime encircled his waist as if he had been wiping his hands on his own skin. The jar of peanut butter stood open and a screwdriver with peanut butter coating its tip balanced across the top.

"Hi, Brad," she said softly.

"Hi, Annalee." His voice was equally hushed. "Can you tell a five-sixteenths wrench from a three-quarters? Hand it to me, will you?"

Annalee did not see Brad again until days after he had returned from the race. By then her eyes were swollen, she had lost five pounds and she dreamed of low, heavy clouds.

Annalee was in a new element.

Over the next two years, the courtship of Bradford Perkins and Annalee Michaels evolved a repeating hourglass shape. From September through the wild, wet winters Brad would be solicitous. Not one to disclose his feelings verbally, he would shower Annalee with time and attention. Annalee would pretend to listen while Brad explained the mysteries of fuel injection or the way to co-opt airplane technology to motorcycles. They swept aside tools and manuals and shared Chinese take-out and pizza on the metal workbench. Brad landed a job as a mechanic at Gary's Automotive Repair and Annalee found work as a cashier at Vera's Market.

If Annalee's parents were dismayed because their eldest daughter was dating below their perceived station, their reserve was ultimately overcome by Brad's nearly anachronistic courtesy. He quietly arranged for his grandparents to meet Rachel and Cooper and introduced them formally in the Michaels' living room. Rachel, always anxious, was eventually relieved to know that Annalee was safe from the social maelstrom of San Francisco where, without Brad, she surely would have drifted back as an antidote to the social lethargy of San Amaro. If she married a blue collar worker at least she would lead a prosaic and thus sheltered life. And at the time Cooper and Rachel's full attention was focused on their other daughter. Evelyn's progress toward adulthood was taking a dark course. It began with shoplifting, then a horrifying arrest for possession of methamphetamine and a brief but terrifying runaway episode. After a long midnight discussion about Annalee's future, her parents stepped aside.

Annalee monitored the approaching bottleneck in their romance. It would come in March when the northern California winter winds and lashing rain abated. Then their relationship would stall. Brad would forget plans they had made. Distracted and often vacant-eyed he would appear to be listening to an inner messenger, and showed lessening comprehension of Annalee. He would repeat himself as if he had become deaf to his own voice. Then his gaze would lift and lengthen, from Annalee to the workbench. The workbench to the books. From the books back to the tools which he would lift experimentally and gaze upon. Then one afternoon in mid-March the stripped-down motorcycle frame would appear with its innards spread in pieces on the workbench. Brad's span of silence and inactivity was broken and obsession flooded in.

From that point until the speed trials in mid-August Brad would be present in form but unavailable in heart and mind. Annalee developed dark circles under her eyes, cried periodically and felt an almost constant chill. She knew that she craved this element in the same way she needed Brad's attention. She never again mentioned accompanying Brad to the races and stayed home for the week before that August morning when he joined his father and grandfather on their journey east.

They were married on Annalee's twentieth birthday in a ceremony that began, almost from the moment of planning, to portend distress for Annalee. She dreamed of a Renaissance ceremony and pictured herself barefoot in a gauze dress with a crown of lavender. Evelyn—who by then could not be counted upon to appear —would accompany her in yellow voile. She imagined Brad in a hand-stitched suede peasant shirt with bell sleeves. A meadow with a towering oak on the outskirts of town would be the setting with Cooper and Rachel, and Brad's grandparents and parents, in denim. If her marriage retained its pattern of alternating distance and intimacy, still . . . she could keep that vicarious immersion she craved and know that Brad would return to her in September.

It was Brad who suggested a tuxedo. When both families met for the wedding rehearsal dinner Brad announced that his racing days were over. Until he was earning a decent pay rate he would not indulge in the demands of the racing life. He smiled shyly at Annalee who consciously arranged her features to reflect pride. In the end they were married in the nondescript San Amaro Community Church with the Reverend

Peters, who always looked disheveled, presiding. The bride wore white, Brad's grandmother's fabulous antique wedding ring suite and an expression of bewilderment and dismay.

Chapter 4

The Oxymoron

It was as if a storm had been gathering during the early days of her marriage, Annalee would later say.

For the first few listless years she kept doldrums at bay as she and Brad drifted in the calm waters of small-town life. Whom to invite for dinner, what to bring to baby showers. Without his own motorcycle, Brad accompanied his father to the salt flats once and spoke in monosyllables for weeks thereafter. Those peaks and valleys that came with the seasons flattened to a single line.

"Honey, couldn't you just work halfway as hard on your motorcycle? Not put so much time and money into it?"

"It doesn't happen that way, Annalee. It's not a weekend hobby. It's all or nothing. And if I can't get out there and push past the rest of them, it's nothing."

Annalee imagined a light in his eyes guttering and flickering out. In turn, her friends saw that same flat expression reach her own features. Although she never discussed it aloud she grieved for the thrill, never to be experienced again, of metaphorically capturing the coattails of someone in pursuit of a quest and being pulled along for the ride.

After two miscarriages the couple quietly set aside any desire for children.

During that time, one shift changed Annalee's very identity. The transformation was independent of her marriage and began with a raucous meeting in the women's sauna at the gym. She was wrapped in a towel, stretched out on a sweet-smelling pine bench when another woman entered. Annalee moved over to make room and they settled in for a meditative sweat. After a few moments her companion said, "Want to streak the men's sauna?"

"What?"

"It's great fun. You run in, whip off your towel, yell 'woo hoo, boys' and race out."

"Are you joking?"

The woman sighed. "Yeah."

Annalee fanned her face with her hand and peeked at the newcomer. She appeared to be in her early 30s with spiked black hair, a square jaw, strong hands and muscular legs.

"I mean, you wouldn't dare run in this place," the woman added. "The floor's slippery as snot. You'd kill yourself. Anyway, my name's Ivy."

"I'm Annalee."

"I know you. You're the cashier at Vera's Market. You were a year behind me in high school and then you married that darling motorcycle guy we were all drooling over."

"I've seen you somewhere too."

"You've seen me in a station wagon piled high with little boys and dogs, and I work over at Home And Garden Land. You and your husband come in there all the time...."

Within a week Ivy had helped Annalee land her job at H.A.G.L. From there, the Duchess of Kitchenware and The Princess Of Complaints forged a solid friendship.

In the second decade of her marriage Annalee noticed a subtle shift in her husband's mood. He brightened. Although he worked longer hours, sometimes on weekends, and he spoke less and often seemed impatient with her, the light in his eyes occasionally flared. By now many of her longer-married friends had divorced and rejoined the singles scene. Only the vows forged in her parents' age group seemed immutable. In her own generation, only she and Ivy and, of all unlikely people, her sister had found enduring relationships. Evelyn had landed in Albuquerque, New Mexico with her vast collection of antique clothing and a tow truck driver named Cliff who appeared to be smitten with her.

Colorless though it was, Annalee was grateful for the stability of her marriage. So she thought.

The cascade of ill fortune began on a morning in October. Brad had left for work. Annalee was opening the windows to permit the distinctive aroma of ripening grapes from the surrounding vineyards when the phone rang. She answered to a woman with a soft, child-like lisp.

"Annalee? You don't know me. My name ith Aura. We need to talk."

For a reason she couldn't name, Annalee felt tendrils of dread snake out from her solar plexus.

Aura talked. She was a beautician. Her salon, Classic Trends, was across the street from Gary's Automotive where Brad worked, she whispered, and she would watch him. "He always looked tho, I don't know, hungry. One day I brought him my home made pie, thtrawberry and apple like my mother made . . . ."

"Get to the point."

The point was, Aura had been sleeping with Brad for the past three years. Aura had just seen her pregnancy test. And Aura was pregnant with Brad's child. "You'll be taking off the wedding rings now," she said. Her lisp had vanished and her voice was undercut by harshness. "Brad don't love you no more. Them rocks are gonna be mine."

When the conversation ended Annalee sat at the dining room table for a long moment. Then the rose. Until dusk she worked. She washed her husband's clothing in the hamper, dried and folded them. Then she opened their closet and pulled down his shirts, his sole tie, his work overalls. She brought packing boxes from their storage room and was adding the last of his belongings when she heard the rattle of his diesel truck in the driveway.

"Aura called," she said when Brad came through the door. "She had a lot to say."

He stood for a moment, looked at the floor and rubbed his hands as if they were cold.

"Even if you wanted to save our marriage," she began. Brad looked hopeful as if he believed a confrontation might be averted. "Even if you tried. Even if I wanted to try, we'd end up the same as all the rest. No late-night talks, no couples counseling, no trial separations, nothing will save it. By the time something like Aura happens the rot is too deep. Just go, Brad." Annalee pointed to the boxes stacked beside their bed. "And by the way, no." She held out her left hand. "I'll sign the divorce papers if you send them. But these rocks, as your mistress called them, are mine."

Later that evening after Brad had left, Annalee went to her parents to break the news.

Her father Cooper roared with outrage and sympathy for his daughter. "That goddamned Brad! We accepted him as a goddamned son! He sits right here at this goddamned table with the rest of us on Thanksgiving and all the goddamned while he's . . . ."

He threatened a lawsuit, he punched the wall, his face was purpled and sweating. And then he clutched his chest and cried out in pain.

At the hospital, Cooper's solemn doctor notified Annalee and Rachel that the ambulance had arrived with moments to spare. And, he said, Cooper's myocardial infarction was simply speeded by his son-in-law's reprehensible behavior. It would have happened eventually, probably soon, because Cooper courted death. As the grape crush approached at this time each year, Cooper would anticipate disasters to the wineries, each involving some failure of his own design. There were never the explosions or gushing leaks resulting in untold thousands of gallons of pricey Cabernet and Merlot flowing through the streets of San Amaro. But it's the frail nature of human beings that our bodies respond to anticipated stress as if the stress were real. Cooper, with his florid imagination constantly presenting images of winery chaos, had succumbed to his own fantasies. Stress had led to heart disease, the need for change was critical and Cooper must retire at once if he valued his life. He must slow down, relax, still the voices in his head, cease grinding his teeth as he slept. Turn off his perpetual mental disaster movie in which his metaphoric airplane is going down and the pilots are all incompetent idiots.

Once out of intensive care, from a hospital bed in the living room Cooper supervised as Rachel packed their belongings and Annalee helped. The Michaels were leaving for a retirement condominium in the vacation Mecca of America, Las Vegas.

Annalee agreed with their request. If anything positive was to come of this double disaster—Bradford's perfidy and Cooper's near-death experience—it was a fortuitous rescue for Annalee. She could return to the family home, be surrounded by loving memories, never go back to the tainted apartment she had shared with Brad. And, incidentally, maintain the house rent-free. Cooper would not sell. Soon, he fantasized, those goddamned doctors would let him resume life back in San Amaro.

⁓

Everyone talked about Annalee's situation. Even the men gossiped. "That Brad, thinking with his little head when the big head should have been running the show," they smirked. The women shared guilty delight. They sidled past Aura's beauty salon, Classic Trends, and then traded information. Perhaps, they conceded, Aura might seem superficially fetching to someone with superficial taste... that aroma of Patchouli wafting from the folds of her retro batik skirts, her blonde braids hanging down to her waist, each one ending in a gold bead. And those small feet in sandals that laced up to her knees, and that tiny frame beginning to swell with pregnancy. But a hippie beautician? What sort of oxymoron was that?

The women of San Amaro flocked to Annalee with aid and advice and hidden agendas. They helped her move her belongings back to her parents' from the formerly conjugal apartment, secretly hoping for a glimpse of Brad, perhaps a confrontation. They fingered her vases and lamps, looking for obvious wedding gifts and wondered if Annalee would now throw them against a wall. Mostly they fished for disclosure. They brought chilled Chardonnay with tender brie and crisp pears, or room-temperature Pinot Noir with mushroom and artichoke spread. The more rich, delicate and exotic the food and wine, they believed, the more likely Annalee might be tempted to offer confidences. In her parents' living room the women sat on either side of her, leaning forward. One or two risked an arm briefly around her shoulder, a hand patting hers, anything to open the floodgates of confidences. What had Brad said? Had she suspected? Would she meet someone new, show Brad she was over him? What about the men she met at H.A.G.L.? It was the perfect place to start a romance, they advised. All men in San Amaro and the surrounding countryside came there for plumbing, household and auto repair supplies, lumber, tools, the things men needed. But even with the lubrication of local Zinfandel, Annalee offered no insight. After several months the visits dissipated and the flow of wine dried. Annalee refused invitations to parties, barbecues, outings where she might be introduced to single, available men. Brad never asked for the wedding rings and she did not offer them. Instead she wore "the rocks" as a barricade and a statement. She was unavailable.

Those most distant from her eventually withdrew. After five years only her mother and Ivy persisted in their dreams for Annalee to find love and romance and, in their minds, happiness.

Chapter 5

What Happens In Vegas....

Annalee was leaving for four days to attend her parents' fiftieth anniversary party in Las Vegas and her boss Marvin was escalating into panic.

"How can you leave now, Annalee? We have twenty toasters coming in and you won't be here! You know how prone these things are to starting fires." He raked his hands through his sparse halo of hair. "Customers will be ranting and raving, their houses will be burning to the ground and you'll be gone. What am I supposed to do?"

"Marv, the toaster fires were two years ago. The factory packed them in excelsior instead of Styrofoam peanuts, remember?"

Marvin ignored her interruption. "Why do your parents need you in Las Vegas for four days? It's an anniversary party, not a Papal conclave. I don't see why . . . ."

"Marvin, breathe. Tomorrow is Friday and it's New Years eve, right?" Marvin nodded but his chest continued to heave. "That's not a big shopping day. Saturday is New Years and we're closed. Nothing can happen if we're closed. There are never problems on Sunday because everyone is in church or sleeping off their hangovers. If there's a complaint on Monday I'll deal with it when I get back on Tuesday."

"You could meet some guy in the airport and you'll think, 'hey, why should I worry about those poor shmoos back at H A.G.L.! I have four days off.' Then you'll have coffee with him and then dinner and next thing you know you never come back."

"What's a shmoo?"

"Or your parents will introduce you to some guy and it will be the man of your dreams."

"Curb that imagination, Marv. There is no dream and I'm not going to meet anyone."

"It will happen," he concluded ominously. "Some day. It's bound to happen."

⁓

Annalee awoke two days later on the first morning of 1990 to the desert sun of Las Vegas. It slipped through her window on the tenth floor of the Tropicana Hotel and flamed from the tiny runway of channel-set diamonds in her wedding rings. The room was silent. After a moment she exhaled, stood to walk across the room and faced the window, exposing full breasts with dark nipples. Heedless of showing them to the world below, she looked down into the Tropicana parking lot. She saw a couple with their arms around one another, hunching into the desert wind. They're probably laughing, she thought, from the tilt of their heads. He's probably cheating on her. Then she drew a breath and turned quickly, that sudden motion of someone who has reached a decision. She strode to the bathroom where, hooked insecurely over the doorknob, was an expensive-looking yellow silk blouse.

Her parents had presented it to Annalee over dinner the night before, a quiet New Years eve at their home on the north side of the city. They sat silently, watching while she felt through the tissue and lifted a corner of the garment.

"Can you just wear it for us at the party tomorrow, honey?" her mother asked, breaking the hush. "It's an occasion. Just a little color, to bring out the blue of your eyes?" Her face held that yearning sweetness as if Annalee were an anorexic who is deliberately starving herself to death while her parents plead for her to take one tiny bite of nourishment.

The garment was of a color lighter than lemon but darker than cream, chemise-cut. At the edges of its dolman sleeves, precise hand-stitching in thread slightly darker than the fabric provided an exquisite touch of detail. Otherwise, the blouse was plain in the way quality clothing is plain. Its statement was made in its texture and in the way it moved and flowed.

Annalee heard the wind slicing around the corner of the Tropicana and heading off toward Glitter Gulch in the far distance. She fingered one corner of the fabric and closed her eyes to appreciate the buttery sensation on her fingertips. In the end, with five minutes to spare, she compromised. Her parents loved her, she reminded herself. And they depended upon her, although this was never mentioned. Of their two daughters, only Annalee still carried the banner of stability and socially appropriate behavior. She dressed in her levis and boots, averted her eyes from the bathroom's full-length mirror and tossed the blouse over her head, then tucked it into her jeans and slipped a belt through the loops. That accomplished, she added a cracked flight jacket, black worn nearly to gray, that might have belonged to a World War I aviator and zipped it. The rim of the yellow silk at her throat would be a gift to her parents. By now they would be awaiting her in the restaurant downstairs. Then she took the elevator to the first floor.

The Tropicana buffet was crowded with well-dressed retirees, tourists in Bermuda shorts who appeared determined to dress for summer vacation even in the raw chill of the desert winter, racing children and dewy-looking couples. Noisy though it was, Annalee could hear her father's voice rising and falling over the talk and clatter of dishes. She followed the sound to her parents at a table in the far corner of the restaurant. She smiled at the incongruous sight of them. Her mother wore an eggshell white running suit with a complement of silver jewelry and flawless cosmetics. Her father wore a blue uniform with gold epaulets, gold buttons and gold stripes along each leg. A blue hat with a gold band and black visor was perched on his knee. Even after five years Annalee was still not fully accustomed to seeing her father in his new role. Cooper Michaels, once owner and manager of legendary Michaels Viticulture in San Amaro, was now the supervisor of the Tropicana Hotel valet contingent.

The transition had taken place only weeks after her parents' move to Sin City. Annalee, who understood her father, knew how keenly inactivity would have pained him so she wasn't surprised when he called to announce a new career in defiance of doctor's orders.

"So your mother and I go to the Tropicana to check out the craps tables," he said. "And here comes the so-called parking valet. The kid mumbles, he won't make eye contact, a shifty-looking thug if I ever saw one. He'll probably steal the car. So I ask for a different valet. The next one smells like dope. The one after looks like a Mafia hit man. And I'm supposed to give these characters my car keys? Are you kidding?"

So, Cooper said, he parked the Crown Victoria himself, strode in to the lavishly-appointed Tropicana management office and demanded to organize the slackers, slouchers and low-belted incompetents in the Tropicana employ. Annalee imagined that the administration was so overwhelmed by his tirade, they had no words to refuse.

"And the hotel says I'm making a difference. The kids hold their shoulders back now. And they call each other 'ma'am' or 'sir,' even each other, which is more than I asked for. And I'm damned if I'll let them smoke anything within a two mile radius." Cooper added that they complain about his bellowing and there was a brief rumor of a walkout, but no one disputed that their tips had increased.

Right now he was shouting at his wife.

"So the woman comes to Vegas to put on one lousy show, and can she pack her clothes like a normal person?"

"No, dear," Rachel said absently. "Try to relax. Remember what the doctor said."

Cooper shot his wife a black look as Annalee kissed the top of his head and then her mother's soft cheek.

"No," he went on. "She can not. She has to bring a bus the size of Cleveland and park in the loading zone. So I find the road manager and I ask him what the hell he thinks he's doing." He looked up at his daughter. "Sit down. Where the hell is the waiter? Where was I? The goddamned parking lot goes to the end of the universe. Why the hell do they have to park in the loading zone?"

"This is a buffet, dear. There aren't waiters. Do you want me to bring you melon slices or melon balls?"

Annalee slid into a chair between her parents and tilted her head toward Cooper. "Whose road manager is he yelling at now?" she asked her mother.

"That woman with the hooters," Cooper supplied loudly. "You don't have to have talent in this town any more. Just a couple of bazookas like watermelons and right away you can park in the loading zone."

"You know, dear," Rachel told her daughter. "That country and western woman? The one with the wigs and all the square dance costumes?"

"Dolly Parton? He yelled at Dolly Parton's road manager?"

"I don't care what you look like," Cooper said. "You can't park in the loading zone."

"How are you, sweetie?" Rachel asked, leaning toward Annalee. "Did you sleep?"

"Of course she slept," Cooper answered. "For what they charge for a bed, you'd damned well better sleep. Anyway, she slept better than she did on that Japanese torture contraption your brother gave us." Cooper reached over to gently pinch his daughter's cheek.

Usually Annalee slept on a futon at her parents' condo where she appeared every four months so that Cooper and Rachel could verify that she was well. But this visit would coincide with the anniversary party and turmoil reigned at the condo.

"You'll stay at the Tropicana," Rachel had told Annalee over the phone. "Your father gets a discount since he's on the staff so we figured, it's such an occasion, what if our girls share one of those fancy luxury suites? I'm so glad Evelyn finally agreed to come. It would be fun for you two to be together again, sharing a room like you did...." Her voice trailed away as if she had already abandoned hope of Annalee's enthusiasm.

Annalee glanced over at the buffet and quelled an episode of nausea. In her past visits she had practiced a peculiar illusion. Unable to steel herself for more than a day to the relentless superficial vigor of Las Vegas, she would craft her itinerary to give her parents the impression of a two-day visit. She always left San Francisco International Airport at 11 a.m., just as the fog was rolling out under the Golden Gate Bridge. She would land at McCarren Airport in Las Vegas at around 1 p.m., spend the next 24 hours with her parents and take the noon flight home. Since this visit was special she had agreed to stay longer. Now she felt doomed by the additional hours of casinos and cigarette smoke, capped by the impending party that night.

After breakfast Annalee returned to her room, replaced the yellow blouse with a black sweatshirt and found the Avis rental desk downstairs where she rented a car for the afternoon.

The drive back to the airport was arduous but decreed by her sister who had acquiesced to making an appearance at the party but only on her terms. There would be no parental scenes at the airport, no criticizing her lifestyle, and she would select her own accommodations.

Eventually Annalee found the Southwest Airlines gate where the passengers from Albuquerque were deplaning. The crowds were slim on New Years day. Finally all but a few stragglers had filed into the arms of their waiting parties or vanished among McCarren's banks of noisy slot machines. Characteristically, Evelyn was the last to shuffle along the ramp. She preferred a seat in the tail of the plane, believing there would be no children there. Annalee saw her sister's mass of red curls bobbing down the ramp behind a man who was pushed in a wheelchair by a steward.

Although they had sporadic telephone contact, Annalee and Evelyn had not seen one another for seven years. Annalee noted that her sister's shoulders were more stooped. This characteristic wasn't dramatic in a woman of 38 but it was a change and Annalee guessed this physical attitude would worsen with age. She doubted that her sister took calcium supplements or cared about such distant concerns as osteoporosis. Evelyn's skin was slightly pallid and her hair, the identical color of Annalee's, was less burnished, less alive somehow. She carried a backpack over her shoulder and she wore hiking boots, dusty jeans that made her appear as if she had just come in from the badlands, and for some reason best known to Evelyn, a lurid red silk cowboy shirt with white fringes, a' la Dale Evans. When she reached her sister, Evelyn slung her bag to the floor. "Hey, how ya doing?" she asked, while her eyes darted. Her shoulders and jaw were tense.

"Calm down. Mom and Dad aren't here. Where's Cliff?" Annalee in turn glanced nervously toward the now-empty arrival gate, scanning for the boyfriend's ever-present oilskin jacket and shag haircut under a greasy Australian bush hat.

"He's not here either. And how about *you* calm down."

Annalee sighed. "You're not on anything, are you?"

"Oh, fucking A," Evelyn said. Two men who had been talking in low voices near the window glanced at them and looked away. "You are such a tight-ass."

"Off to a great start, Evelyn. Thirty seconds after landing and you've already mentioned fucking and my ass."

Evelyn grinned. "Hey, that's a pretty good biological inventory even for me." Her expression flattened. "Look, my goal in life is to survive this anniversary circus. That means cruising somewhere above it without slitting my own throat or someone else's."

Annalee couldn't help herself. "Ev, what's the reason for this hostility? You act like our parents fed you nothing but moldy apples and changed your diapers every third Thursday. I have a feeling you tell your Narcotics Anonymous buddies that you were abused."

"Now you're going to start ragging on me about being in recovery."

Annalee turned away. "Let's just get in the car and find whatever place you found to hole up."

⁓

Annalee's sister was silent for the drive to Bennie's Bungalows. They parked in a dusty lot. Evelyn swung her legs out, stood and looked around with a slight smile at the row of squat cottages. A single car with its left front wheel propped on a cinder block was the only other vehicle. She walked away toward an office and came back moments later with a key.

Inside the dim room, Annalee commented, "Smells like mildew in here. And something else. I don't want to know."

Evelyn reached into her backpack, withdrew a bottle of Seagram's and two shot glasses and sat on the bed. "So," she said, "Dad got another job that suits his temperament."

"He's doing OK."

"Yeah, well." Evelyn's rapid-fire speech accelerated even more. "Maybe he is. But I got to tell you, 'Lee. After all those years of eating Rice Krispies for dinner while he forged his little empire in San Amaro I'm having, like, an issue as you say in California with Dad parking cars for a living. What happens next? He has another heart attack and they move to Bumfuck, Idaho where he can get pissed off about potato farming?"

"He's happy, Ev. Leave it alone. He's made a stand-up routine out of being the valet umpire. Tourists use the parking service at the Tropicana just to see his shtick. He can shmooze with the tourists and yell at the valets at the same time. And he doesn't have to hold back. If anything it's probably keeping him from having another heart attack. Plus he and Mom get to eat at the Tropicana and go to the shows for free."

Evelyn poured two full shot glasses, handed one to Annalee who eyed it suspiciously, then delicately sipped at the top of her own.

"Come to mama," she said. "Oh, that's good."

Annalee settled into a vinyl-covered lounge near the window. The chair appeared to have been left outside at some point in its history. Patches of grime showed on its armrests and along its back as if someone had tried to clean it and gave up. She sniffed the whiskey.

"And you drink this stuff?"

"Yes, for medicinal purposes and I'm one sick puppy, remember? Oh damn, look, Annalee, I'm sorry as hell. Are you still feeling like shit? Is it still the pits?"

"It's . . . ." Annalee began.

Evelyn, who had lit a cigarette and was exhaling loudly between her teeth, interrupted. "I wanted to come out and be with you when Brad left but you know me." She grinned.

Annalee replayed the scene she had watched in her imagination even in the first hazy weeks of anger and shock. Evelyn materializing in San Amaro, perhaps with Cliff whose tendency was to offend and then apologize before he could be confronted. Evelyn on alternating doses of cocaine and heroin, her moods rising to a pinnacle of mania and then swooping down to nodding serenity alternating with wrist-to-forehead depression. For whatever emotions Annalee felt at the time, Evelyn would have outdone her in quantity, decibel level and demand for succor.

"I would have killed the both of them. How the hell did he ever hook up with some commune refugee named Angina?"

"Aura."

"Did you meet her? Mom heard she got excommunicated from Morningstar Ranch or Wheeler or one of those places out in your area for being a nymphomaniac when she was only twelve years old. Who ever heard of getting kicked out of a commune for doing the nasty? You could probably get the ax for *not* fucking the cult leader but . . ."

"I have no interest in her," Annalee interrupted. "Do you want to go over to the folks's place? Mom is making brunch in honor of your appearance and then all hell is going to break loose before the party starts. We need to clear out before the caterers arrive."

"OK, I'll change the subject. I'm just trying to say, I felt really bad when it happened." If nothing else, Evelyn's expression showed genuine concern. "Mom says you're on some sort of widow trip." Evelyn eyed her sister, inhaled and let the smoke out in a stream while Annalee gazed over her shoulder and wiggled one foot. "You're hiding behind those wedding rings. They give you a wall a mile high. Why don't you pawn the fuckers? I could use the money if you can't. What's up with that? And moving back home?"

"Moving back home had nothing to do with me and Brad."

"Cut the crap. You could go in, dust the heirloom television and do a few laps around the ancestral palace without living in it. If you want to regress to your childhood you could at least go back to San Francisco where there's some culture." She snorted. "San Amaro!"

"I have a job and friends in San Amaro, Evelyn. Brad left, I didn't want to pay for the apartment myself, the house was empty . . . what's the problem with my going home? I mean going back to the folks's place?"

Evelyn blew cigarette smoke toward the window and leaned back on the pillows. "Lee," she said, her voice softening. "You can't bullshit a bullshitter."

For an instant Annalee was tempted to confide her fear of the misery she would inevitably endure in a new relationship. Her perceptive little sister was not the best listener but she didn't hold back when she had a point of view. Then Annalee played out the probable course of events after an unburdening. Evelyn would enmesh herself in Annalee's life, repeat her secrets to Cliff, probably try to match Annalee with one of her Narcotics Anonymous cohorts from Albuquerque. Talking to her sister would provide the sort of comfort Evelyn usually found for herself. Immediate gratification and then long, complex efforts to escape the consequences.

Chapter 6

Another Match

It was the night of her parents' anniversary party and Annalee was being stalked. She first sensed the shadow at 8 p.m. just after the arrival of the early guests. The back of her neck prickled and she felt a need to monitor her peripheral vision. By 9 her intuition was confirmed and at 10 she was in full rout. Her pursuer was Mrs. Corinna Krasney, a slender woman in a cerise caftan, apricot coiffeur and white boots. She materialized now by the buffet table, now engaged in too-animated conversation, then lifting a canapé to her coral lips between manicured thumb and forefinger, never making eye contact with Annalee but drawing ever closer. At her side, his biceps encircled by one bejeweled hand, was an attractive, muscular man with sandy hair. Annalee sighed.

"You remember our neighbor Corinna Krasney," Rachel had said last month. "Her son will be visiting and she might bring him to the party. It will be nice for you to have someone to talk to, with nothing but us old people around."

"Let me guess. He happens to be single."

"You'd have to ask him yourself. Now Annalee, shall I hire decorators or try to arrange the ambience myself? I'm thinking maroon, white and gray . . . ."

Mrs. Krasney honed in while Annalee who'd had too much to drink—"too much" being six ounces of Chardonnay indulged in a private narrative about the pursuit.

"The age-old dance of predator and prey unfolds on the savannah," she intoned to herself. "Mother lion and her cub encircle the hapless wildebeest. The doomed animal raises its head and tests the air, sensing danger." Annalee dilated her nostrils while she monitored the approach of her pursuers. Mrs. Krasney's strident coloration made her easy to spot. The other guests—her parents' old friends from San Amaro and newer associates from the Tropicana and the neighborhood—were more conservatively attired, many of the men in starched shirts with ties and the women in their little black dresses. "The high pampas grass parts to reveal the lions' stealthy approach," Annalee recited silently. "The wildebeest is cautious and moves away." Annalee dodged into the downstairs guest bathroom where she sat for several moments on the closed toilet seat cover. The lavender-scented room spun gently. Annalee was not so intoxicated that she couldn't count the number of hours remaining before her return flight the next afternoon. Fourteen hours. Then she splashed a handful of water on her face, careful not to spatter the yellow silk blouse. "The cool waters of the Zambezi provide a brief respite," she murmured.

After several moments she opened the bathroom door and peered out. Her tracker wasn't visible and she took two steps intending to slip into the crowd. Immediately her senses were stunned by a nearly palpable cloud of Giorgio as Mrs. Krasney appeared at her side. Up close, Annalee saw that the son was a John F. Kennedy look-alike. He was about 45 with layered hair, fair skin with a wash of freckles over his nose, and hazel eyes. He was tall with broad shoulders. Probably sells overpriced computers, Annalee decided. She smiled a thin smile at Mrs. Krasney and switched her inner voice to a nasal east coast twang. "Annalee, this is my golden son Shmendrick," she parodied silently. "He's just getting over a divorce. It wasn't his fault. Will you marry him?"

"Annalee," Ms. Krasney said, "I'd like you to meet my son Jerry. Jerry, this is Cooper and Rachel's daughter Annalee from California." She patted her son's arm, almost imperceptibly pushing him in Annalee's direction. Then she released her grip, returned Annalee's smile and strode away toward the sour cream and spinach dip.

Jerry and Annalee stood together in the throng. "Annalee," Jerry murmured, holding out a hand. As she reached to shake it she noted a ring tattooed around his right pinky finger. She stole a long glance. It was a filigree of intricate design, reached nearly to his knuckle, was obviously designed by a master and its creation was probably quite painful for Jerry. Not a computer salesman, then. She covertly wiggled her left ring finger to wink her diamonds.

"Is that white wine you're drinking?" Jerry asked. "Shall I refill your glass?"

A sudden stirring from the direction of the foyer rescued Annalee. She wasn't tall enough to see over the crowd but Jerry stared.

"What on earth is that woman wearing?" he breathed. "She looks like a cross between Morticia Addams and Madonna." Annalee felt a sinking sensation. It could only be Evelyn. "And where did she get that guy? It must be Crocodile Dundee on acid."

Damn, Annalee thought. Cliff must have come in on the noon flight from Albuquerque. That would explain Evelyn's absence all afternoon while Annalee helped with the party preparations. Rachel and Cooper, obsessed with food, drink and décor, scarcely noticed when their other daughter vanished after their perfunctory, near-silent brunch.

"I have a small emergency. Be right back," Annalee lied, and slipped from Jerry's side. Then she paused in indecision. If she intercepted Evelyn and Cliff she'd condemn herself to monitoring them all night to prevent them from causing chaos. But she had no means of escape. Cooper had picked her up earlier in the Crown Victoria whose back seat was loaded with borrowed salvers and flatware from the Tropicana kitchen. Perhaps she could slip into the hall and call a taxi. Yet, guilt stayed her course. She couldn't abandon her parents.

She moved closer and passed guests who were sidling away from the door. Now within sight of Evelyn, Annalee noticed that her sister had exchanged her cowgirl getup for a deep purple floor-length velour gown with a high pointed collar and a train. Its sleeves extended to end in gloves. Annalee was momentarily captivated, having never seen a piece like this. Over the gloves her sister wore a silver ring on each finger and thick silver bracelets that looked like shackles. Cliff smiled vacantly into the room, nodding at the far wall. Annalee took one full bracing inhale and moved in from the side, intending a surprise approach. But she was spotted.

"Ladies and gentlemen," Evelyn cried. "The wild, sweet union of Cooper and Rachel—God, what a disgusting idea. Anyway, this union which we celebrate tonight has brought about these two fruits of their looms." She paused and looked confused. Cliff raised his empty hand as if in a toast. "Those fruits," she went on, "are myself and the lovely black widow who now appears before you, my devoted shister . . . sister, Annalee."

Evelyn stepped forward and lost her balance as the train of her dress wrapped around an ankle. Annalee caught her with one hand on her shoulder and another around a violet-clad velour elbow. Cliff reached over to hug her. " 'Ay, it's the big sis!" Annalee was never certain if his Australian accent was feigned or authentic. He grinned wetly and winked one reddened eye under his swagman's hat. An aroma of pot wafted from one of his many pockets. Annalee saw that he had lost an incisor since they met seven years ago.

A hush fell over the party crowd. Those closest to the threesome were silent but a murmuring began on the periphery. Annalee felt a cascade of protectiveness. First, toward her parents who would surely be shocked and embarrassed. For all of their many years of travail and struggles with Evelyn's unpredictability they maintained the illusion that she would somehow come to her senses and change. And Annalee felt loyal to Evelyn herself. She knew from experience that her sister would be frozen with sincere remorse in a dozen hours when the drugs and alcohol in her synapses sizzled out. Annalee turned to block their view from the guests. Her first priority was to extricate the couple. She could decide on a course of action later.

"Hey, guys," she said. "I have something to tell you. But it's a secret. Let's go out."

"Annalee has a secret, ladies and gentlemen!" Evelyn made no move toward the door. "But don't worry. I'll come right back and tell all you wonderful people. And first, a drink. Waiter," she cried. "Where the hell are the drinks?"

Most of the guests pretended to ignore her while others gaped.

"Drinks, drinks, I come bearing beverage!"

Startled, Annalee turned to see Jerry Krasney holding high a bottle of wine in one hand and the long stems of four goblets in the other.

"Let us drink a toast!" Jerry cried. He strode past the trio and through the front door.

"That's me man," Cliff said. He turned to follow with Evelyn teetering on his arm. Perplexed and grateful, Annalee brought up the rear and closed the door behind them.

Outside, the night was silent and the desert air was dry, a sensory contrast to the perfume, heat and hum of the party. Cooper had lit a small chain of tiny lights that lined the pathway from the street through the front yard with its gravel and cactus arrangements typical of Las Vegas residential areas. Midway between door and curb, Evelyn and Cliff drained their glasses. Jerry sipped and Annalee discreetly poured her wine onto the base of a saguaro and offered it a silent apology.

"You are a prinsh among men," Cliff slurred, beaming at Jerry. Evelyn gazed at him owlishly.

"Do I know you? Are you my sister's new boyfriend? You better not be another one of those bucking fikers. No." She giggled. "Fucking bikers like Brad. If you hurt her I'll kill you. My sister is having a very hard time." She reached out to pull Annalee close and kissed her cheek.

Annalee sighed. "Evelyn, Cliff, this is, uh, Jerry. Jerry, meet my sister Evelyn and her boyfriend Cliff, from New Mexico." She stopped. She couldn't offer the customary introductory biography of a man she didn't know. "His parents live next door" would have seemed inadequate. But in any case, Evelyn and Cliff were obviously not stable enough to participate in social niceties. And, Annalee reasoned, given Jerry's split-second ability to size up the situation he probably wasn't expecting ordinary behavior. She wondered if he was a social worker.

Jerry stepped into the silence. "Nice party, huh? But the food sucks."

Annalee stared at him. Her parents had spent next months' mortgage on the food and beverages. The silver trays displayed authentic New York lox, tiny hand-crafted paté in paper-thin layers of philo, cheeses imported from Denmark and tiers of carved roast, turkey breast and slices of yeasty French bread. The desserts table could have made a French chef swoon.

"You know what I could go for right now?" Jerry said, meeting Cliff's bloodshot eyes. "A hamburger." He drew out the "m" so that he nearly crooned. "A juicy burger with fries and lots of gooey stuff. You think I could find a decent hamburger in there?" He tilted his head toward the party inside.

"No way," Cliff said. "Man, a big ol' burger with pickles and onions...."

Evelyn, still clinging to Cliff's arm, chorused, "A hamburger? In there? They probably just have those little mea'balls on sticks."

"Oh, I know," Jerry said. "Kilroy's! You can't get a better burger anywhere in Vegas. Maybe the world." He rubbed his hands together. "I'm ditching this old folks' home and going to Kilroy's. Hey, would you guys join me?"

Incredulous, Annalee watched this communion.

Cliff nodded enthusiastically and Jerry ushered them all toward a sedate gray rental car parked in his mother's driveway next door.

Kilroy's was a dimly-lit wooden structure. Only two other tables were taken and four men watched a football game on the television over the bar. This being Las Vegas, no one seemed interested in the entrance of a redhead swathed entirely black except for a yellow silk blouse, accompanied by a woman in an antique purple gown on the arm of a disheveled hippie in Australian garb, and a man who would have looked natural teaching a graduate seminar in English literature.

They slid into a booth, Annalee beside Jerry. Across from them, Evelyn leaned on Cliff's shoulder. Cliff ordered the Kilroy's double decker special with onion fries and a beer. Evelyn chose the Mexican plate and a beer and Annalee asked for a diet Pepsi. Jerry ordered a cheeseburger and fries with a beer, and then called the waitress back for a well-done hamburger with extra lettuce for Annalee who was too disoriented to object.

Except for three occasions when she felt her way to the ladies' room and then emerged sniffling, Evelyn was dreamy and subdued throughout the meal while Jerry and Cliff chatted. Annalee listened in, curious for some hint of Jerry's profession. Perhaps he's in the Peace Corps, she reflected. He segued easily from one environment to another like a man who could be airlifted down into a jungle to pick up a spear and join in a tribal hunt. Or he might be a priest. He clearly was filled with unconditional kindness. He seemed genuinely interested in Cliff's theories about Avis Rental Cars as a front for right-wing extremists.

Annalee searched her mind for some recollection of whether priests always wore clerical collars and if they were allowed to drink beer. Eventually Cliff wiped up the remainder of his burger drippings with a bite of bun. "That 'it the spot," he commented.

"Guess we should head out." Jerry glanced at his watch. "Where are you guys staying?"

Evelyn looked quizzical. "Weren't we going back to the party?"

"Party?" Jerry echoed. "Oh, you mean Rachel and Cooper's party. It's probably over by now. I didn't see anyone who looked as if they could stay awake very long." He reached for his keys with one hand and the check with the other.

Or a Green Beret, Annalee thought. One of those professions where you develop razor-like intuition and can jump into any action.

"I don't know how to thank you," Annalee said as she and Jerry pulled away from Benny's Bungalows. Then she wished she had begun differently. She had an idea of how he might wish to be thanked. "That was nothing short of an act of heroism. I'm amazed. You knew just how to read the situation and you didn't get to stay at the party."

"Actually, I had a good time. Far as I'm concerned, the evening was a success. Your sister and her friend are interesting and I wasn't having much fun at the party."

Annalee, who was braced to defend Evelyn, was caught short. She mentally criticized her sister but she would never dish about her to anyone else. Now that Jerry wasn't going to analyze her sister she shifted to the next immediate concern. The route back to her parents' took them past the Tropicana if they followed Las Vegas Boulevard south. It was nearly midnight and Annalee desired nothing more than a hot bath and a long sleep until morning. She could call Rachel from the phone in her room and explain her absence which possibly went unnoticed. She'd save her father a late-night trip across town to bring her back to the hotel.

"Jerry," she said, "I really don't want to go back to the party." He nodded in her peripheral view. "I'm staying at the Tropicana. Would you mind dropping me off there? The folks have a cleanup crew so they don't need my help and there can't be much left of the party by now."

"Sure. Nice place, the Tropicana."

Jerry's hands on the wheel were strong but not muscular. The ring tattoo hinted at a counter-cultural lifestyle. He didn't comment on Evelyn's behavior so chances were he wasn't a psychiatrist. Something about him didn't seem businesslike, Annalee reflected. A computer aficionado might not have been so firm but fluid in coping with the Evelyn-and-Cliff traveling circus. Perhaps he was a bartender.

"Just what *do* you do," Annalee asked, as if she had been musing aloud.

"Me? Oh, I'm the scum of the earth." He grinned over to meet her quizzical expression. "I'm a defense attorney. I work in Amarillo, Texas with a bunch of irreverent, impoverished, dedicated folks who represent mostly poor people. We have a nonprofit legal agency out there. That means we're up on the roof patching leaks ourselves when we're not trying to get innocent people out of jail."

As they approached the Tropicana, Annalee's anxiety increased. Perceptive Jerry must sense that if her parents' celebration was a success it was owed in a small part to his rescue. And, sensing this, he would expect something from Annalee. At least a drink at the bar. And then would come the inevitable course of events. She would yield to a romance with him. Once they were involved she would start waiting for phone calls that would never come or disclosure of some sort of aberrant behavior. Or he'd cheat on her from the outset. He probably had a coven of underpaid legal assistants competing for his attention. A man this humble and attractive? She allowed herself one more peek at his profile and then turned to watch the lights of Vegas. Now Jerry was pulling up to the Tropicana. With her father off duty tonight the valets were somnolent. Before one of them could drift over and demand the car keys, Annalee had grasped her purse with her left hand and the door handle with her right.

"Jerry, great to meet you," she said. "Thanks for helping." The door latch made a quiet snick as she opened it. She swung her legs out and stood, then leaned down and smiled at Jerry. "Enjoy your stay in Las Vegas." He opened his mouth to speak but Annalee straightened and closed the car door. She walked swiftly behind the car and headed for the wide glass entryway with a firm stride and her chin up as if she were being approached by a mugger. As the hotel's doors slid open she was alert for the next sound. When she heard the slight hiss of tires as Jerry pulled back into traffic and left, she felt relief. And an annoying undercurrent note of disappointment.

Due to a flight delay and then a four-car pileup on the Golden Gate Bridge, Annalee didn't cross the threshold to home until nightfall the next day. Later, flossed and brushed and creamed for the night, she opened her travel bag to put her things away and found a small folded sheet of note paper, the kind her mother kept by the telephone to jot down reminders of meetings and social events. On it was a telephone number with an unfamiliar area code and, in Rachel's handwriting, "Jerry." Annalee thought back. She had left the bag on her parents' kitchen table for only a few moments. Rachel must have been lying in wait to plant the phone number. Annalee wadded the scrap and tossed it overhand into the wicker trash basket in her room.

Chapter 7

Embarrassment

Annalee let herself in through Ivy's unlocked back door as usual. From the living room she heard the voice of Ivy's sister Sharon.

"And are the parents worried?"

Typical of women who are gossiping or discussing sensitive medical ailments, Annalee thought idly as she crossed the kitchen to join them. They never use pronouns or common names. *The* parents, *the* bladder, *the* menstrual cycle, *the* husband won't shower at the gym because he's so sensitive about *the* penis.... Then she heard Ivy's voice.

"... don't see how they can help but worry. Rachel knows there's more to the story."

Rachel? They were discussing her parents? The topic must be Evelyn.

"... tried to fix her up with a neighbor's son at the party. He sounded like a nice guy and he's an attorney."

Annalee stopped.

"And I suppose she found fault with him?"

"He could be Jesus Christ and she'd have a problem with guys who wear sandals."

Annalee winced, feeling more annoyed than betrayed. Of course Ivy talked about her. Everyone talked about her. But she believed her best friend would be less brutally honest.

"I'm telling you, Sharon, I don't know if it's worth bothering."

"Look, just let me try. You invite her over and say it's to help paint the deck. I'll show up with him and we'll leave the rest to fate."

"I hope he doesn't still have those sideburns. And what if he starts talking about sperm?"

"The man doesn't discuss his job every minute, Ivy."

Annalee's imagination stalled at the image of a man with sideburns—she saw him with his collar turned up and an Elvis-like sneer—involved in a professional activity that involved ejaculation.

"And for that matter I hope *you're* not going to talk about sperm. One little joke about semen and she'd be out the door in a heartbeat."

Annalee tiptoed to the living room and stood unobserved in the doorway. She saw Ivy on the couch with a beer and Sharon in a rocking chair, holding a teacup.

"Well, at least he's got job security," Ivy said. "He travels to cattle ranches everywhere, doesn't he, even Italy. The ranchers think he just rocks when it comes to artificial insemination. Hey, that's funny. Rocks, testicles, get it?"

Annalee rolled her eyes.

"Still," Ivy went on, "I can't see her dating a man who spends his days up to his armpits in cow vaginas and jacking off bulls and his Saturday nights at the Elk's Lodge. It won't impress her that he's a Third Degree Lord High Antler-Bearer or whatever they're called."

Annalee, still leaning silently against the doorjamb, thought she knew the sound of an elk call. She produced one now, cupping her hands around her mouth to produce a long, wavering honk. The result, while inaccurate, was gratifying. Sharon screamed, leaped from the rocker, spilled her tea and stumbled over an ottoman. Ivy lunged for her sister but caught only air. Sharon regained her footing and two pair of eyes turned to the doorway to meet Annalee's gaze.

"When's my wedding? I'm so looking forward to prancing up the aisle on the back of a heifer with my intended awaiting me at the altar, wearing those rubber gloves that go up to his elbows...."

A month later on a Sunday morning Annalee received a telephone call from her mother.

"Annalee, I'm worried about Evelyn." Rachel was perpetually worried about Evelyn but instead of her breathless, dramatic tone her voice was puzzled. "I called her last week about those shoes she wanted? Cliff said she was over at a friend's. Then I tried later and Cliff said she was getting the oil changed and there was a long story about the carburetor.

I call again and again and each time Cliff answers and gives me some complex excuse. She never calls back and it's strange for Cliff to be answering the phone."

Annalee immediately phoned her sister. Cliff answered.

"Cliff, it's Annalee."

"Sis! Whassup?"

"Nothing much. Put Evelyn on the line, would you?"

"Evelyn? Oh. Well, see, Annalee, the wash machine busted. There's water all over the floor. I'm mopping up and Ev's gone to the Laundromat. We was washing all the blankets and sheets so I don't know when she'll be home. The laundry's across town, see, and all the university kids from . . . ."

"Cliff?"

"Yeah?"

"Where's Evelyn?"

"I just told you, man. You should see the mess in here. I wouldn't be surprised if our washing machine falls right through . . . ."

"Cliff!"

"Ok, look Annalee, just don't panic."

"I'm not going to panic. I'm going to calmly crawl through the telephone line into your living room and throttle you. Where. Is. My. Sister!"

"Oh fuck." He sniffed and then Annalee heard the muted, clotted sound of tears.

"Cliff? Are you crying?"

"Evelyn got busted."

"She got *what?*"

"Busted. It's like when the police come and . . ."

"I know what 'busted' means. What the hell is going on out there?"

"Man, I am so freaked. Ev's locked up and it ain't fair but I got a felony on me record so me word don't mean nothing. Fuck, man, I don't know what to do." Cliff sobbed.

At least the man could cry. Even through her alarm Annalee's opinion of him shifted slightly toward the positive. She softened her tone.

"Do you think you could stop calling me 'man?' It's disorienting. Just tell me what happened."

"They come in here with about a hundred cops and six dozen drug-sniffing dogs and said we was growing pot. The rent is in her name so they went after her."

"Were you growing pot?"

"Well, yeah. But the thing is, they didn't find no pot. Just two seeds I left on the coffee table. Them dogs must of had allergies. They never smelled the plants up in the attic."

Annalee heard Cliff strike a match and inhale.

"I hope that's just tobacco."

"You think I want to end up in the slammer too? They probably got the place bugged. Man, I mean Annalee, I hauled them pot plants down to the dump and shoved 'em over the edge. Then I got rid of everything else. Rolling papers, bongs, crack pipe, spoons, pills . . . ."

"I get the picture."

"I must of flushed the john a million times. I am so freaked, I ain't slept since it all come down."

"If they didn't find plants, how could they arrest her for growing them? That doesn't sound legal."

"One of the cops says they was up in a surveillance plane and seen them in the back yard. Seems our cunt neighbor called 911 and reported we was growing drugs. She's on the rag because I park me tow truck in her driveway when I come home for lunch. There weren't no plants in the yard but forget the law being any help. They give her a public offender. The way things are around here they could send her up for twenty years. She'd get five even if they just convict her of possession for the seeds." Cliff sniffed and blew his nose.

"Oh my God." Annalee's fingernails dug crescents into her palms and her heart crashed in her ears. "How much money would she need for a private lawyer?"

"Forget it, Annalee. None of them douche bag scum-sucking lawyers within two million miles will give her a fair trial. They all go out drinking with the judge, then arrest innocent people. Bunch of hypocrines."

Annalee stifled a mental image, framed in *National Geographic* orange, of prehistoric creatures that could be hypocrines bathing in ancient Lake Tanganyika.

"Cliff, why didn't you call me?"

"Oh, yeah, sure. That's all Ev was hollerin' when they put her in the cop car. 'Do not tell my folks,' she was yelling out the window. When I seen her in jail she made me promise. She says your dad will have another heart attack and your mom will have a stroke. She thinks you already got a negative attitude about her. She's going to kill me for talking to you now."

"Sit tight and try to keep Evelyn calm, OK? I'm not sure, but I may have an idea."

"I love you, man."

Annalee paced the length of her mother's yellow-trimmed kitchen. Her sister was in jeopardy. She imagined Evelyn huddled on the floor of a jail cell, her feigned hardened exterior splintered with fear. In her mind's eye Annalee saw Jerry's profile outlined in the neon lights of the Las Vegas strip as they drove through the night. She remembered his words. "I'm an attorney. We have a nonprofit agency . . . trying to get innocent people out of jail."

Annalee fished Jerry's number from the trash, braced herself and called.

"And you say the cops were in a surveillance plane, Annalee? That's interesting. Look, next week is clear. First thing Monday I'll head out to Albuquerque and see Evelyn."

"Oh, no Jerry! I didn't want you to go to that kind of trouble. I just wanted to get your opinion, maybe some referrals."

"Albuquerque is only a few hours away and this sounds fishy. Cliff is right about the twenty years. Law enforcement in New Mexico is frustrated because they can't catch the big guys, and Evelyn could be a scapegoat. They have no evidence that she was growing so someone is lying with or without the seeds. It's right up our alley. I really liked your sister and Cliff, and my hunch is they're going to be scared out of any more pot growing."

Annalee anticipated a long wait. She had never been involved in a criminal case but from television and novels she knew trials could take months. So she was stunned a mere four sleep-deprived days later when a jubilant Cliff called and began talking without preamble.

"That Jerry is a fucking genius, Annalee! She's out! Jerry got her acquitted! We just now come home. Man, as soon as she walked in the door she must have taken a shower for ten hours, then she ate a ton of salad, then she cried, then she slept for about a week, I could hear her crying and laughing and singing in the shower, now she's sleeping again!"

"Fantastic!" Annalee sunk to the floor, nearly weeping with relief. "How did he do it?"

Cliff stopped talking to light up, then she heard a slurping that sounded much like someone drinking from a beer can. "It was fucking incredible. He gets the cop on the stand and he starts asking about that-there surveillance plane."

"Like the airplane is a suspect in a lineup?"

"Right. Then Jerry drags out this flip chart and starts talking about fix-wing aircraft." Cliff stopped to guffaw and slurp. "Then the cop starts saying, 'well now, what I meant was blabbity blah.' But Jerry proves there's no way you can see a plant in someone's yard in the middle of a city from that high up in that particular plane."

Annalee found herself thinking in cosmic terms. Fate had brought her Jerry. He had rescued her family from embarrassment and chaos at the party and within weeks he became the one person she could turn to in a situation that left her dizzy with helplessness. He was attractive, he was the right age, his values were solid. He led an interesting life. Annalee imagined sitting proudly in the courtroom as Jerry stood before a judge, pounded his left fist into his right palm and cried, "incompetent, irrelevant and highly immaterial!" She wondered what Jerry might be like in bed. She replayed the touch of his hand as they met at the party. One touch opened the door to all touches, all possibility, all pain but also all pleasure. She felt adrenalin course through her veins. She could phone him. She could regret it. But she could be cherished again, feel that sweet sense of security. And, thank God, put an end at last to the incessant matchmaking. Jerry would never leave her for a retro bimbo.

An attorney who worked with poor people would be stable, solid and mature unlike the childish biker Brad. For a week Annalee rehearsed, abandoned the thought, returned to it. She imagined Mrs. Krasney and her mother high-fiving in the driveway . . . an unlikely scenario but yet, her mother might succumb to that much exuberance if she knew her daughter was safe in another man's arms at last.

Ultimately nothing remained but to call Jerry. Annalee tried to sound neutral as she thanked him for rescuing Evelyn.

"You don't need to thank me, Annalee. Evelyn did so much thanking we couldn't keep up with her. She and Cliff drove the distance to my clinic the day after she got out. Cliff rotated everyone's tires and checked our oil and radiators, and Evelyn typed, stapled, licked stamps and envelopes, made coffee, hugged and kissed me and everyone including the guy who came to fix the telephones."

Her self-absorbed sister showing gratitude? Annalee set the anomaly aside.

"Jerry, actually I called to . . . ." Annalee could feel the receiver nearly slip from her hands and a rivulet of sweat rolled down her wrist. She determined to keep the tremor from her voice. "I called because I was wondering if you'd like to . . . . " That was not how she intended to begin. She glanced at her notes and found the letters swimming like fish in a turbulent sea. "I called to say that it might be nice to see you again." Not quite right, but adequate. "I visit my parents often. And if you go to see yours maybe we could visit that great hamburger restaurant, Kilroy's." Now she was babbling. "You know, where we went with Evelyn and Cliff? No big deal. I just liked the hamburger." It was not elegant, but the deed was done. She waited.

"Annalee." It was just one word, her name, but in the softness of his tone Annalee knew this call had been a mistake. "I know your parents. They're not racist."

Of course they weren't. What was he talking about?

"But my mother, unfortunately, is. I'm sure she manipulated your folks into getting us together at the party. She's relentless about breaking up my engagement with Kuwanayama."

Was he speaking in tongues? Maybe he was in one of those cults where they wave snakes around.

"You seemed so disinterested in me, I didn't think I needed to explain that I'm engaged. My mother is threatening to boycott the wedding next month. It's so ironic, with Mom having been the senior librarian for all her years in New York City and Kuya starting a library for the Hopi nation, trying to introduce literature to the Hopi and Navajo children, bringing them together in a way they can relate...."

OK, so little Kuya would get the Nobel Prize For Library Work. Would he ever shut up? After what seemed like an eternity Annalee finally thanked Jerry again for saving Evelyn, wished him all the best in his marriage, they hung up and she glanced at the clock. Less than five minutes had elapsed since Jerry had answered her call. But it was time enough.

After years of passive irritation, a new emotion at last provided the impetus she needed for action. Annalee was embarrassed.

Chapter 8

The Plot

Annalee emerged from the garage with Ivy's copy of *Alaskan Bachelors,* retrieved unopened from the recycling bin. She made her way up the stairs and down the hall, passing Rachel's sewing room—formerly Evelyn's bedroom—and stood for a moment in the doorway of Cooper's study. While it was understood that no room in her parents' house was off-limits to Annalee, she often felt like an intruder in this wood-paneled interior. It was so steeped in her father's presence that she believed she could smell his aftershave and the aroma of forbidden cigars. Normally she crossed the threshold only to dust the shelves, write the occasional letter or pay a bill. But now she entered, placed *Alaskan Bachelors* face-down on the desk and crossed the plush dark rug to open a closet.

Under a stack of file folders and other detritus that remained of her father's working life, she unearthed The Ollie Machine, her father's paper shredder, so named after infamous shredder Oliver North. Cooper had used it to shred clients' financial statements, contracts and other confidential material on the many nights when he brought Michaels Viticulture home from the office. The machine was cumbersome and Annalee struggled to horse it over beside her father's La-Z-Boy. Then she removed the cover from a floor lamp so that it would cast a direct 150-watt light. She resisted an impulse to draw the blinds. This was not, she reassured herself, pornography.

She opened the magazine midway and scanned a profile of a gold miner named Klute whose description included a direct quote. "I would like to meet a lady with good breast's." Evidently the wishes and hopes of each *Alaskan Bachelor* were proffered verbatim. Annalee imagined an editor, wearing a green eye shade and sleeve garters over a full Arctic thermal body suit, with fingers too cold to excise the wayward apostrophe.

She flipped back to the cover and gazed down at the man in the red ski parka. Dimples formed soft commas in each cheek and auburn hair jack-knifed in a smooth, glinting sheath over his forehead. A man who uses hair styling products in the Alaskan wilderness? Too self-absorbed. Probably watches his reflection in every store window he passes. Or did they have stores? In every frozen puddle. Annalee reached for Ollie's on-switch, the machine rattled to life and Annalee fed it. One strip of the shredded front cover missed Ollie's debris receptacle and slid to the floor between Annalee's feet. The man's blue eye looked up at her. She removed it to the trash between thumb and forefinger. On to the actual profiles. Annalee inhaled and began.

She found the hopefuls presented chronologically by age, youngest first, and began to shred all men younger than 40. Her chosen one should have lived long enough to incur the requisite slate of angry wives, illegitimate children, prison commitments, and unresolved emotional and financial baggage. She started with the fresh-faced Jarred, age 19, and ended with a 39-year-old pipeline worker named Beaver. With a dozen profiles remaining she reached Ronnie Dean, age 41, minister of the Uganik Church Of Our Lord in the frigid necklace of the Kodiak Islands.

Ronnie was bundled to his chin and faced the camera on skis. He invited any woman between the ages of 18 and 60 to join him in the leadership of his congregation. Behind him was a small frame structure topped with a cross. His two pale daughters at his side squinted into the distance. Ronnie didn't explain what had happened to his wife. Annalee examined the background but did not see a mound topped with another cross. No, Annalee decided, for two reasons. He probably wasn't evil enough to fit her standards and she would never give false hope to a man with children.

Chester, age 46, held aloft a rifle in one hand and in the other a bottle of beer. An unkempt mustache bracketed his wet grin. Layers of cold-weather outerwear didn't hide a belly that extended in a fleshy shelf above his belt. He sought women "for romance and ??? Ladies older than 21 need not apply." His shredded image mingled with that of the preacher and the red parka.

Sanders tugged at Annalee's heart. He was burly with a full beard, thick neck and solemn brown eyes. Although he was surrounded by towering banks of snow, he wore merely a lumberjack Pendleton shirt over a turtleneck with jeans and boots. His reddened hands held an ax and he stood with one foot braced on a stack of logs. Sanders wrote of the echoing nights of loss and missing his wife, dead in a car crash three years before he fled Minnesota for the Alaskan wilderness. His eyes were sad and his lips down-turned. Deserves a sincere woman, Annalee thought, and fed him to Ollie.

Donovan of Barrow was forthright about his appearance. Owing to a genetic defect he stood a mere three feet tall but, he said, he had a good sense of humor. A school bus driver who wrestled the wheel of an antiquated vehicle across black ice from late August through June, he lifted weights to meet the demands of a job which sometimes required him to jack up that leaking dinosaur and change a tire in a blizzard. This professional skill gave him a massive chest and shoulders in troubling visual contrast to his attenuated legs. For a hobby he raised sled dogs. Annalee gasped when she read his animal training theory. "I believe in beating my dogs," he commented before he vanished into the Ollie maw. Not even as a joke, she thought, would she allow an animal abuser into her life. Perhaps it was a typo and the shivering editor had omitted the word "not," but she decided not to take a chance. The entire venture was risky enough.

She shredded Army sergeant Marcus, stationed near the Arctic Circle, whose wife approved of threesomes and who was poised to send air fare, one-way only.

And the silver-haired John, not his real name, who allowed only the back of his head and left ear to be photographed for reasons which he would explain to the right woman. Someone so paranoid would see through her ruse.

And she shredded Conrad who had come to Alaska two years ago seeking his fortune, found Alaska to be a mistake and hoped to marry a woman with her own home in Florida or Texas.

Annalee needed a believable stooge and only four profiles remained.

Then she flipped another page and felt a small percussion, as if each door and window in her parents' home had been opened and then slammed. The house seemed to fall silent.

Russell Lee—Rusty to his friends—stood balanced on the pontoon of a blue floatplane that appeared as fragile as a dragonfly on a clear blue lake. As if in knowing contrast to the mounded parkas and sheepskin of his *Alaskan Bachelors* peers he was shirtless, wearing blue jeans belted just below a dark line of belly hair. He held with both hands, at the level of his navel, a fat glistening fish. It looked slippery and wet. Annalee's jaw slackened. Water dripped from the fish down Rusty's legs and onto his bare feet. His photo showed even white teeth and shaggy ash blonde hair, shoulder length beneath a sailor's cap, and green eyes behind aviator glasses a' la John Denver.

Annalee rose from her father's La-Z-Boy, slipped *Alaskan Bachelors* face-down on the floor and wandered to the kitchen to brew a cup of tea. Returning she read that Rusty, age 45, was a bush pilot in the harsh bowl of the Alaskan interior. He was a transplant from Georgia who had come north as a young man to satisfy his love for flight. Annalee imagined the stutter of a small plane's engine and a splash of pontoons touching down on water. The room seemed to bob gently around her. Russell Lee was the perfect candidate. He was 3,000 miles away, he was unknown to her matchmakers, he was the right age, a pilot which upped the ante on romantic appeal, and he wasn't bad to look at. He was the man of everyone else's dreams. Annalee would catapult those dreamers into excesses of romantic fervor. And then she would reveal the truth about him. It would be easy to find. She squinted at his photo for a sign of malevolence. She saw nothing suspicious but sociopaths were often charmingly attractive. "OK, Russell Lee or Rusty to your friends," she murmured. "You're on." She tore out his profile and shredded the remaining pages.

Next Annalee read *Guidelines For Meeting an Alaskan Bachelor*. It required submission of a three-page questionnaire and came with a warning. "Over 96% of our men say they would not respond unless you include a picture and personal note." Annalee wondered what precise number was over 96% and then curbed her sarcastic monologue as she made her way to the attic. For the next hour, amid the dust and cobwebs she rifled through Evelyn's discarded collection of treasures from San Francisco consignment shops, hitch hiking journeys along the Pacific coastline and forays to Canada and Mexico. She unearthed an antique blouse, a bustier, a velvet hat with short veil and a pair of soft, tight Levi's worn to a silken gray with wear showing on the knees and the round imprint of a tin of Copenhagen chewing tobacco on the rear pocket. Dressed in this costume she added boots, dangling earrings and lip gloss, then headed to the one-hour portrait studio in the next town where her image was captured with her back to the camera, hands in her rear pockets, one breast in high profile, looking over her shoulder with a mysterious smile. An inviting image, Annalee thought with satisfaction, but tasteful.

That evening Annalee stared at a blank notepad and wondered what would be appealing to this Rusty stooge. She couldn't feign an interest in fishing. Even the sight of a freshly-caught salmon in the butcher's cooler at Vera's Market made her queasy and she couldn't distinguish a hook to catch trout from one meant for marlin. But a pilot would seek a woman who was unafraid of flight. Annalee enjoyed air travel, so she could be authentic about that claim. Holding hands by a fire, cliché but necessary even if the fire was the only means to avoid death by hypothermia. And the requisite walking in the moonlight. No, wait, no walking in moonlight. Who's going to be walking around out there at night? Freeze your butt off....

⁓

"Dear Rusty,

"As soon as I saw your picture in *Alaskan Bachelors* I wanted to meet you. I love your smile and the romantic look of you standing on the airplane, holding that luscious wet fish.

"If you were here right now you would see a slender woman with red hair and blue eyes, looking at you from a desk in a room with redwood walls. It's winter in northern California so her boots and umbrella are always handy. She lives in a house north of San Francisco and works in a funny hardware store where everyone wears a crown and has a royal title. She is mature but playful and has a good sense of humor. She likes air travel and holding hands by the fire on long winter nights."

Annalee erased the last four words. They probably had a fire blazing away on short summer nights as well.

"She imagines you smiling the way you do in your picture but she can't imagine how you live. Are there bears? Is it cold all the time? Your picture looks warm."

Annalee stopped and edited the last word. She would not succeed in this façade if she stayed in her comfort zone.

"Your picture looks hot.

"Now she is putting her own picture in an envelope to send to you so that you can look at it while you write back to her. She hopes you do...."

After completing the questionnaire—age, address, phone number, occupation—at last she bundled the documents into an envelope. Then she drove to the post office and pitched the package into the mail chute, rendering it impossible to retrieve and feed to Ollie before it headed north for the settlement of Garnet, population 300, somewhere north of Fairbanks in the middle of Alaska. She fantasized Ivy's excitement as they shared pages of Rusty's letters in the H.A.G.L. staff lounge, how the news of the romance would course through the information arteries of San Amaro, feeding the rumor mill, quickly reaching Las Vegas where her mother would begin to plan the wedding reception. And then the secret thrill of satisfaction when she disclosed the heinous truth about Rusty. She should start now to interview private investigators. It might be expensive to send one to Alaska but if necessary it would be worth it for peace at last.

Even when she was married Annalee never enjoyed Valentine's Day. Brad wasn't a sentimental man—at any rate, not with her—and the day usually passed unnoted. In 1990 it fell on a Wednesday when the usual H.A.G.L. customers were joined by men wandering the aisles with dazed expressions. On Thursday, a day of returned gifts that ran to plumbing tools and kitchenware, Annalee came home an hour after her usual time and fell asleep on the couch. The ringing of the phone brought her up through cottony layers and she answered before she was fully awake. Ivy had gone to the movies with her family so the caller would be her mother.

"Hi, Mom. Have you talked to Evelyn?"

"I've been called a lot of things but nobody's ever called me Mom."

Annalee didn't recognize the man's voice. In the background she heard a hollow moaning and a hissing that seemed to approach and recede like a wave. "Oh, sorry, I thought you were my mother."

"Let me look. Nope, I'm nobody's mother."

"Sorry. I was asleep. Who is this?"

"Asleep? I bet you look cute in your sleep. You sure do in your picture."

Although his voice echoed as if he were calling from the depths of a well, Annalee could hear the inflection of the deep South.

"What picture? Who are you?"

"You sure are one cute redhead, little lady."

"Little *lady*? What century are you in?"

"Hey, you'll fit right in. In Alaska we like feisty redheads who wear tight blue jeans."

"Alask.... Wait. Holy cow, are you Rusty? Oh my God, that's right. I put my phone number on that questionnaire. But actually I didn't expect you to call."

"And actually here I am. Happy day after Valentine's Day!"

Mail, just mail, that was all she intended. Distant and cool and easy to control. A voice in her ear was too shocking, too intimate. Too close. Annalee grasped for words. "Well. Hello, Rusty. Uh. That's a nice little airplane in your picture."

"Hello yourself, Annalee. That's a nice little butt in your picture."

"A what?"

"A butt. I like your picture. You have a really cute butt."

"Wh.... Are you joking?"

"I never lie about a lady's butt."

"That is outrageous!"

"Wait, are you upset?"

"Of course I'm upset."

"Why? What's the matter?"

"You are so crude!"

"Crude? Well now, hang on here a minute. How come you're all pissed off?"

"I don't even know you, and you just call me up out of nowhere and start talking about my . . . about my behind."

"Heck, lady, it was you sent me the picture of it."

"I did not send you a picture of it!"

"What is it, then, one of those fake posters of some movie star and you stick your head through it and your ass is really ten feet wide?"

"Oh my God!"

Annalee slammed the receiver back in its cradle and sat wide-eyed with her palms pressed to her chest. The phone rang again. Annalee gingerly lifted the receiver. Once again she heard the susurrus that spanned the distance 3,000 miles north.

"Look, can we start over? I didn't mean to get on your bad side. In your picture you looked like you were fun so I just thought it would be OK to tease you but I guess you're kind of tense. It's OK. Some women are like that."

"Some *women* are . . . ." Annalee stopped and consciously slowed her breathing. She would need to make allowances if this façade was to work. She softened her voice. "I just felt that it was rude of you to talk about my behind." Annalee briefly gritted her teeth. "At least not until we get to know each other." She tried for a giggle which sounded hollow.

"Well, what do you want me to say now?"

"You could apologize."

"If you want me to apologize, I do. I'm not sure why, but I do."

"It doesn't count if you're not sure why."

"What?"

"If you don't know why you're apologizing then the apology is invalid."

"Are you always like this?"

"I'm just trying to explain."

"I thought you wanted me to apologize."

"You have to know what you're apologizing for."

"Jesus. I give up. Lady, you are way too uptight for Alaska. Stay in California so you can buy granola with food stamps and smoke pot and walk around barefoot all day."

Before she could frame a pithy response the connection ended and she heard only a dial tone. Miffed, she strode to the desk and rifled through papers until she found Rusty's profile. No telephone number was offered. Annalee stalked upstairs to floss and brush, then slipped under the covers and glared at the ceiling. Too uptight for Alaska! Just because she lives in California he accuses her of being stoned and not wearing shoes. It was too annoying. In fact, she would set the record straight. She reached for the phone, called directory assistance for Alaska and asked for the operator in the town of Garnet. The number rang 15 times before Annalee gave up. She imagined a woman sleeping at an antiquated switchboard under mounds of blankets and fur as a brace of bears and a gale outside batter at the door of her cabin.

When Annalee was upset she would clean the house. She was soothed by the warmth of running water on her wrists, the hum of the vacuum cleaner, the focus away from whatever beset her. When the chores were finished she would feel refreshed. Thus she rose early the next morning after a night of intermittent sleep. The man had called her tense and assumed she was on Welfare. She of the soft voice and calm demeanor, who worked hard all day amid grime and grease. She strode to the kitchen where she faced a tall china cabinet. On its shelves, behind its panels and in its velvet-lined drawers was a 12-person setting of silver, Doulton china, Waterford crystal and other accoutrements of fine dining at the table of Rachel and Cooper. They must be polished and rearranged.

To think, he didn't know why he should offer an apology.

Annalee glared at the saucers and matching cups, fragile as petals. That photo was not in any way meant to direct attention to her behind.

She stopped and gazed unseeing at a stack of soup bowls. No. The photo was light-hearted and humorous, exactly as she intended. She lifted a porcelain goblet, its luster so white that it seemed translucent, put it down, then took it to the sink and rinsed it. Just his voice alone. That accent cried out "National Rifle Association." His father probably voted for Wallace. In fact, he would have been of voting age in 1972 when Wallace ran for president. Maybe *he* voted for Wallace. So yes, she was guilty of stereotyping too, she allowed, but she was correct in her evaluation of him. He on the other hand was so, so wrong. Annalee replaced the goblet, then realized she hadn't dried it. Of course she was not tense. Just the opposite. Like this lovely vessel she was simply delicate, a quality which could be misinterpreted by a man with all the grace and sensitivity of a goat.

Annalee crafted a letter in her mind. She would express her irritation. No. she would be cool. No, that would convince him of her uptightness. Twice she wandered from kitchen to desk, sat and gazed at the notepad. "I just thought you should know . . . I'm really upset by . . . Why don't you just stick your . . . Perhaps you won't understand women who . . . .

Three days would pass before Annalee no longer started in hope and fear when the phone rang.

Chapter 9

The Visitation

  Home And Garden Land, never a beauty spot in any season, suffered particularly in the muddy aftermath of the late winter rains. On the first morning in March the store was surrounded by a swamp of native red clay. This substance, sticky and dingy orange, adhered to the shoes of customers, staff and delivery drivers who tracked it in and through the building. Their footsteps marked paths from the doors to the aisles to the cash registers. Gritty tire tracks followed the course of T'Angeline Duffy, The Lady of The Forklift, from truck ramp to stock room to shelves and back again.

  Annalee gingerly made her way across the mud-slick surface of the loading dock where her boss Marvin dourly inspected ten new Hoover vacuum cleaners, still in boxes, that had fallen from the delivery truck into the morass.

  "And God looked down upon our land," Annalee said, "and proclaimed, 'I have giveneth the North San Francisco Bay its lovely hills, its rich waters, its towering redwoods.' Ow!" She slipped and grasped a post to right herself. " 'Now, how shall I make San Amaro unique among all places? Oh, I know, I shall bestow mud, yea, and all living things shall be covered.' "

  "You shouldn't talk that way about God, Annalee." Marvin looked worriedly at the sky.

  "Don't be nervous, Marvin. I wasn't being critical. In fact I was appreciating the holy creativity. Just look out there. Spring is approaching San Amaro and with it come our seven varieties of mud. Like the dwarves in Snow White but more wet. We have Sticky, Grimy, Slippery, Sandy...." She stopped as she noticed the young forklift driver,

T'Angeline, who had dismounted her vehicle and was silently gazing at them from a doorway.

"If you're looking for something to do, T'Angeline, start wiping these vacuum cleaner boxes." Annalee tossed a shop rag in the direction of her coworker. "You'd think, Marvin, that missing the loading dock would have been enough. But no. JJ had to pitch them into the LaBrea Tarpit out there." She wished her boss would hire competent delivery drivers instead of his wayward family. His son, Marvin Phee Junior, had been flagrantly incapable and now so was his grandson, Marvin Phee Junior Junior, known as JJ. She pushed a clump of curls from her forehead, basting her cheek with red clay, and added a mud-caked rag to the pile at her feet. "Plus we have those portable milkers with faulty suction pumps. I've had pissed-off dairy people in here all morning." As she reached for a new rag she looked up to see T'Angeline still standing with the rag at her feet. A punk rocker who sported neon purple hair and a row of studs in the cartilage of each ear, T'Angeline often appeared to be lost in philosophical thought when she was merely lost, but at the moment her expression seemed to communicate rapture. Her kohl-lined eyes were wide and she had caught a maroon-colored lower lip between her prominent upper teeth.

"What's wrong with you, T'Angeline?"

"There's a man here to see you."

"Is he holding a suction pump? I could just scream."

"No."

"OK, then did he say what he wanted?" Annalee swiped at mud spatters on a crate and transferred mud to her black Levi's.

"You."

"T'Angeline, sweetie, could you give me the short version of this conversation?"

"He .... Wow."

Annalee wiped her hands on a rag and tossed it to the pile. "OK, my little space cadet. Let's go put the mystery man out of his misery. Whatever he wants from The Princess Of Complaints, it's not going to be pleasant. Let's just hope it's speedy."

T'Angeline turned and walked slowly back to her vehicle as if in a trance. The girl needs less drugs and more medication, Annalee reflected.

As she crossed the stock room toward the sales floor Annalee noted a phenomenon she first identified as an odd sound. She stopped and listened, puzzled, and then realized she was hearing the unfamiliar sound of silence. Other than the hum of a floor heater, the air was unusually still. With each sales island given its own microphone, the temptation for H.A.G.L. royalty to address the multitude usually created an incessant cacophony. Annalee had seldom known an unbroken span without someone's blaring need for a forklift, stock boy, lottery donation, coffee run or answer to 35 across on the morning paper's puzzle. She thought of returning to the loading dock to tell Marvin that the sound system had failed but opted for dealing with the complaint first.

As she passed through the silent store, Annalee felt an odd sense of being monitored. And although her coworkers appeared to be engaged in their work, tinkering with stock and fiddling with boxes, she noticed that their usual bustling and meandering had ceased. Instead they were all turned to face her work station, The Island Of All Returns where a man stood at her counter. Clearly he had created a scene. This was unusual at H.A.G.L. where even the transient ranch hands were polite when they returned defective purchases.

As she approached the customer, in spite of the impending confrontation Annalee's attention was arrested by his air of otherness. He leaned on one forearm with his boots crossed at the ankle and his hands in his pockets and looked directly out onto the sales floor with deep smile lines bracketing his lips. This was not a demeanor typical of someone returning defective merchandise. And he wore a fabulous sheepskin jacket, stitched together in classic patchwork fashion with tufts of brown fur outlining each cream colored patch, the collar high and lined with similar dark fur. Its front was fastened with oval buttons that appeared to be bone. Her sister Evelyn would have coveted this unique garment. But the jacket's construction was secondary to its obvious lineage. Annalee knew the signatures of hard work. The man wore his jacket into demanding situations. Dark lines of scarring crossed the shoulders, the hem was blackened and the elbows gray.

Closer, she saw that the top button showed a bas relief carving of an animal with antlers. Bone carving—wasn't that a folk art among the natives of Alaska? Ignoring the tiny frisson of alarm that snaked up her spine, Annalee walked behind her counter, fixed her reassuring Princess smile and braced for the tale of frustration, the needless round trip from some distant ranch on roads that were little more than cattle trails. However he merely said, "I would like to apologize."

"Not your fault. Bad suction pump? It's a nuisance for you, isn't it? And then you're late with the milking. If it's any help you're in good company. I've seen nothing but bad pumps all day. We're talking to the distributor and we'll give you a discount with your refund. Now if you would give me the receipt...."

Keeping up her soothing chatter, Annalee held out her right hand while she looked beneath her counter for yet another return ticket. Then she stopped. The object resting on her outstretched palm did not have the familiar texture and heft of a sales receipt. It was too large, too cool. Had an artist captured Annalee at that moment the scene would have framed a slender woman with tousled red hair under a faux crown, a smear of clay across one cheek, wide eyes directed to the floor and a photograph balanced on her right palm.

She gaped at him, wordless as he spoke. He had not come from Alaska just to see her. He had flown his Piper SuperCub farther south down the western seaboard to Santa Cruz where, he said, he had some business. As he had roughed out his flight plan in Garnet he saw that it would be a dogleg inland after refueling in San Francisco to the rural town of San Amaro where an interesting unknown woman was angry with him. The intensity of her emotion intrigued him. He'd stop and apologize and possibly learn more. Her photograph was not indecent and he was sorry to have referred to her behind in such a callous manner.

He delivered the news to Annalee with no sign of nervous discomfort. Although his accent was clearly from the south, Rusty evidently was not a man who drawled. He was merely unhurried and spoke as if he and Annalee were discussing points of interest on the landscape.

"I kept getting this picture in my mind of your store," he said, "from your little note. I didn't think there'd be too many stores like this." The man smiled and gestured out into the still-silent H.A.G.L. floor, causing a wave of suddenly broken stares.

"I see," Annalee intoned. She would hear out his story and ease him toward the door. This moment would pass. She thought of dinner waiting at home, stir-fry in a wok, bean sprouts and spinach, some fresh locally-caught salmon.

"So I just stuck your picture into my back pocket when I left. It wasn't much trouble to land over at your little airport and the taxi driver knew all about the hardware store where everyone wore a crown."

"I accept your apology."

"I haven't apologized. I just said I *wanted* to apologize. Will you have dinner with me tonight?" Was he deliberately raising his voice? Her coworkers seemed to have inched closer as if in a body.

"Shhh," she hissed. "No."

"OK, Annalee. You're uncomfortable and I won't bother you any more. But look, here's my phone number." He lifted the photograph from the counter where it lay and wrote on the back. "The last four digits are the same as the tail number on Blue Lady, my airplane," he said, "so if you should just happen to lose this and then decide to give it a shot after all, just look at my picture in *Alaskan Bachelors*. Unless you threw it out." Annalee winced, remembering the profile that remained in her father's desk drawer. "And I really would like to say I'm sorry."

Annalee inhaled to speak but he interrupted her. "Uh-uh. I still haven't said it yet. I'm not letting you off that easy. I have five sisters, Annalee, and two daughters and an ex-wife. I think I know a bit about women. There's something about me that upsets you more than it should. I want to know what it is. If I don't get that chance I'll be disappointed. But I'll let it go." Before she could respond he had turned his collar up, buttoned his top button and was calling out to Annalee's galvanized coworkers. "I am leaving the building! Grapes to stomp, cheese to spread!"

Annalee felt her cheeks flame as the glorious jacket receded in her peripheral vision. She knew what awaited her. The excited rumors had probably spread beyond the parking lot by now. In fact, the telephone was probably ringing at her parents' house in Las Vegas. She abruptly sat on the floor and regarded the stacks of forms on a lower shelf. She had been meaning to take their inventory and now she would do so. Cross-legged on the always-damp concrete, she gazed at the pile of documents until the persistent knocking on her counter let her know that it was no use. She looked up to meet a row of eyes. Ivy was staring down at her along with T'Angeline, Countess Sheila of Drapery Cove and Lawrence, The Bishop Of Bookkeeping. Annalee sighed, stood, brushed the seat of her jeans and followed Ivy to the staff lounge.

When she had crafted her *Alaskan Bachelors* ploy Annalee had envisioned a special role for Ivy. Her friend cared about her and wanted only the best, albeit her own version. She could believe she was helping Annalee make plans for a new life with a new love, feel satisfied that she had done her part to bring it about, comfort Annalee in her feigned sorrow when the relationship proved to be a disaster, vow to accept her friend as single and content with her life. In a matter of a month, possibly two given how slow the mail would be from Alaska, the harmless prank would have run its course, she would have made her point and it would all be over. Now, Annalee knew, there wouldn't be that measured building of interest, the controlled course of events that would set her free.

"So," Ivy said. "The mystery man who loped in from some beer commercial and talked like an Elvis impersonator? 'Ah jes stopped bah ta see thet lovely redhaid that works h'yar, name a' Annalay?' I thought T'Angeline was going to climb into one of those furry pockets and latch on like a baby kangaroo. Why didn't you tell me you met someone?"

"I didn't *meet* him."

"Excuse me?"

"Look, remember that personals ad magazine, *Alaskan Bachelors*? You wanted me to try it out? I was going to play a little joke and pretend to be interested in someone and then he'd turn out to be a jerk. You'd see that all this matchmaking is doomed. So I sent this guy a picture of me and he took it the wrong way."

"What picture? What did he take the wrong way?"

"He said he could see my butt."

"Oh my God. You sent him a picture of your butt."

"I did not send him a picture of my butt. Why do I keep having this conversation? I sent him a picture, OK? It was just a picture of me but he started making all these crude references to my behind."

"What the hell were you wearing?"

"Pants, Ivy. I was wearing pants."

"*Panties* pants?"

"Will you stop it! I was wearing one of Evelyn's old Levi's and I was just standing like this." Annalee stood and placed her hands in her rear pockets, turning to look at her friend as she had in the photograph. "And he misunderstood."

"I'm not surprised. Just tell me. Is he an alcoholic? A lot of guys up there are, you know."

"How should I know? Like I said, I never met him until this minute. But he flies an airplane and you can't fly drunk. So I guess he's not."

"Annalee, haven't you ever heard of a 'functioning alcoholic?' It's just another way of saying the drinker has lowered his standards. My father was one. Went to work every day, attended every PTA meeting, drove all us kids to the movies on Friday night. You couldn't tell he was a flaming drunk except when he was beating up my mother on Saturday night. If you're out in Fuckall, Alaska and he gets crazy nobody will be there to rescue you."

Annalee slapped her palms to her forehead and gazed up at the dusty ceiling of H.A.G.L. "Oh for heaven's sake!" she cried. Then she met her friend's eyes. "Look, Ivy. Maybe I didn't think it through. I was just going to make up a romance, get some guy to write to me, then you'd think I'm moving on. My parents and everyone would lay off the matchmaking. Then it was going to fall apart like they all do. I was never supposed to meet him and he definitely wasn't supposed to show up here. I was just going to have some fun. It was a joke."

Ivy brooded into her Diet Pepsi. "I'm still not sure how making up a romance to satisfy your fan club ended up with The Marlboro Man turning up at H.A.G.L. One way or the other I wish you had included me."

"I'm sorry, Ivy. Let's forget it ever happened. It was a dumb idea."

The women hugged and headed back to the sales floor.

But like that first tiny slip at the start of an avalanche, Rusty's appearance heralded a massive shift for Annalee.

Chapter 10

The Rift

In the weeks that followed Rusty's appearance at H.A.G.L. Annalee was plagued by a curious phenomenon. Alaska seemed to surround her. It popped up like a jack-in-the-box in pictures, references, persistent reminders. Although she had never thought of the place before, now that it had entered her life in its oblique way it was everywhere. At the dentist's office she reached for a *National Geographic* and flipped to a piece about the Masai in Kenya. Then the magazine slipped from her hands and fell open to a spread about the Denali game preserve just outside of Fairbanks. An episode of "This Old House" on PBS, a program she faithfully watched for hardware tips, was replaced with no prior announcement by a documentary about the polar bears of Barrow, Alaska. Even the weather seemed to mirror the theme. In the hours before sunrise an unseasonable late winter frost crept down and over the hills to shroud the San Amaro valley. When H.A.G.L.'s doors opened the vintners and farmers would leave the warmth of their overworked furnaces to troll the shelves for frost remedies and Annalee would hear them murmur over and over, "we might as well be living in Alaska."

Annalee was first bemused, then annoyed, then distracted as this presence of Alaska in her otherwise orderly life persisted. It haunted her peripheral vision and eventually infiltrated her sleep.

She dreamed of sighting down a white embankment with her eyes seeking out the imprints in snow of four-legged prey, straining to find the direction of their hoof prints. She woke, startled into consciousness by the persistent whining of the white, blue-eyed dog that paced next to her bed. Only after she had drawn three deep breaths did she recall that she had never owned a dog and that so far, thank goodness, snow had never fallen on San Amaro. She dreamed of a man standing out on a vast white plain, dressed in shaggy animal skins as if he had come from an ancient culture. His high boots were laced with leather straps and ruffs of thick cream-colored fur lined his hood and gloves. While a dozen sled dogs milled around him he laughed down, distracted by the antics of a puppy. Then he looked up toward a heavy flat cloud that had settled low between himself and a mountain on the far horizon. It was dark on the bottom and flailing with long wisps at its crown high in the sky. Concern crossed his features. Annalee startled from sleep with a feeling of urgency, her heart racing and an ache in her calves as if she had been running for hours. She found the electric blanket and comforter on the floor where she had tossed them to allow the sheen of sweat to dry between her breasts and thighs.

In tandem with her preoccupation Annalee felt a gathering excitement, the kind that precedes action. It was as if that strange frozen winter had become her personal spring.

By the third week after Rusty's appearance, sleep-deprived and unnerved, Annalee made mistakes. Instead of returning an order of defective blenders she sent them back to the shelves. She granted a massive refund for a washing machine that worked perfectly once the "on" button was pressed. When a customer asked to exchange steel bolts for anodized aluminum, Annalee wafted to the shelves and returned with a bubble-pack of assorted rubber faucet washers. She appeared to be stoned. Those who talked about Annalee had a surge of colorful new anecdotes.

～

Pragmatic Annalee's opinion of anything supernatural ranged from wry skepticism to frank derision. She had no patience for Tarot, astrology, channeling or the many other occult trappings of her New Age peers. When Brad left and her coworkers chipped in for a palm reading with Gypsy Psychic Madame Lisa, to see when Annalee would meet a new man, she thanked them and surreptitiously tossed the gift card into H.A.G.L.'s dumpster. So she knew that her unusual mental state had no roots in the paranormal. She wasn't revisiting a past life, afflicted with déjà vu or channeling the spirit of an Inuit elder. She simply felt that her new awareness of distant Alaska, with all of its inaccessibility and challenges and mystery, resonated with some ancient note in her soul. It called to her and finally one night, from her father's easy chair and with Rusty's phone number in hand, she called back. When his machine picked up Annalee said simply, "I feel so strange. Can you just talk to me?" She left her number and then sat musing at the floor, her mind blank, until the phone rang minutes later.

"It's funny," he said when she answered. "I thought I smelled your perfume the other day, the one you were wearing at your store, with your blue jeans and all that mud."

For the next three hours, Annalee and Rusty spoke across the miles. They talked about Alaska, about cold, the shift in the seasons. He was a fisherman, he said, and described a job which had no resemblance to fishing as Annalee knew it. No hooks, bait or lines were involved in this form of catch. While Rusty would circle some 4,000 feet over the Pacific ocean in his SuperCub looking down for the distinctive darkened patches that signaled the presence of migrating schools of herring or sardine, fishing boats below would be waiting for his voice over radio waves. Then, flying low, he would guide them out into the choppy waters, position them over the teeming schools that were invisible to them from the boats, and direct the lowering of nets that could have covered H.A.G.L. The job was unpredictable and dangerous and Rusty described it in the same tone her father would use to describe a day at Michaels Viticulture. He also told Annalee of the caribou that migrate in herds of thousands, and how to manage the seasons, and how so many people come to Alaska with dreams and leave disillusioned. "The day-long darkness in the winter gets to people. By their third year they're heading for Hawaii before the first snow."

Periodically Annalee would try to end the conversation, citing the cost and lateness of the hour. Each time Rusty would simply begin a new thought, drawing her into a life of focused attention to the demands of that distant environment. He described a way of being that speeded her heart and crafted a portrait of independence and self-confidence. When their long conversation finally ended Rusty asked, "why did you call me?"

"I can't explain it, Rusty. Not even to myself."

"Are you coming to Alaska?"

"I don't know. Can we talk more some day?"

Two weeks later at that same hour Rusty called her again. From 3,000 miles away, far north of the Canadian border, he described the annual spring phenomenon known as breakup. Ice, some two feet thick, had begun to shift and crack on the Yukon River and its tributary, the Chena River near Rusty's cabin. The water beneath the ice was warming from the lengthening daylight above and the surface responded to this nearly imperceptible rise in temperature. Ice, he said, was a living thing. In San Amaro ice meant discomfort and, for some, financial ruin. In Alaska ice seemed sentient, responding to seasons and the air, making its needs known in return, oblivious to humankind.

"When the ice gets ready to flow you hear it sighing, like an old man turning in his bed." He said that soon deep fissures would form along the solid surface of the rivers, then cracks, then the ice would begin to bob and move and sometimes scream as the miniature tectonic-like plates rubbed together, as if gathering strength for their route to the sea.

Annalee could hear in her mind the restless movement of that vast ice, feel the trout begin to rise up from their dormant season on the river bottom. And she felt herself move and shift as if, like that hidden force under the frozen surface, she was carried along on a current.

And, he said, "you hear the sound out there, like a tree falling?" The phone went silent so that Annalee could hear trees crashing in the distance. "That's what it is, trees falling. It's the beavers out on the river, cutting down their trees to make a dam. We hear that sound all night long." Annalee thought of the creatures, how very small they were and how impossibly large the trees they challenged and won.

From then on, through the spring, summer and into the fall, twice each month Rusty would call. A rift split Annalee's world and deepened with the passing weeks. There was work and Ivy and her doting parents and all of their yearning concern for her, their wishes and hopes and expectations. And there was her vicarious immersion in a distant way of life that seemed to pull her like a moon pulled the tides. She felt a hunger for these talks. She would take the phone outside onto the deck and watch the glinting stars as they wheeled overhead, and Rusty's voice took her to Alaska. Rarely he asked her for personal disclosures.

Sometimes he talked about his ex-wife or his daughters and sisters and parents who live in Georgia, Oklahoma or Alabama. But each time she would turn the talk to Alaska and he would effortlessly be drawn back. At the end of each conversation Rusty would ask, "will you come to Alaska?" And Annalee would vow to find her voice and choose a day . . . next time.

Likewise, she vowed daily to disclose this astonishing development in her life to her best friend Ivy. She knew she should. She would give up the news the next day at lunch, she promised herself. Or certainly Sunday over the phone, or when they went shopping together on Friday night. And then Ivy would share this bright new facet of her life, tell Annalee's parents and everyone at H.A.G.L. Soon all of San Amaro would know. Annalee cringed from the thought. So the days passed and Annalee never broke her silence. Thus, "the Widder Perkins," whose every act was grist for the San Amaro rumor mill, became a woman with a delicious guilty secret.

⁓

T'Angeline and Corinna, the Countess of Curtains, were whispering near the H.A.G.L. loading dock. Annalee saw them do a double-take as she came to shake out a dust mop, and then saw T'Angeline whisper, Corinna nod and look sympathetic. With eyes downcast, the little forklift driver glided to Annalee's side and touched her shoulder.

"Thought I should tell you," she said.

Now what? No doubt another dishwasher had fallen from the truck and the unit would need to be sent back to Chicago. It had happened twice this month.

"I saw your ex-husband Brad with Aura in town last night," T'Angeline continued softly. "And unless Ms. Woodstock Throwback is gaining weight only in her belly it looks as if she's pregnant again. I just wanted you to hear it from someone who cares about you. I'm so sorry."

Annalee squinted. Brad? Oh, right, Brad. Two more beats passed as T'Angeline and, from a distance, Corinna waited for Annalee's sob, the tightening of her lips and the self-protective rounding of her shoulders.

Instead Annalee turned to look at her coworkers with an expression of something like wonder. "Thanks," she said. "Thanks."

Annalee went to the staff lounge and sat musing into her tea. For five years her public role as an abandoned wife had been like a controlling lover. It sheltered her even as it held her hostage. Now it was dissipating like the morning fog. Who would she be without the protective cowl of her loss?

"So," Rusty said as their conversation wound down on the next Saturday night. A sense of anticipation, like those living creatures with scales and gills beneath the frozen water, rose in her consciousness. He said the words. "Will you come to Alaska?"

"Yes. Next week."

If the two could have seen one another in that moment Annalee would have marked Rusty's eyes wide behind his aviator glasses. And Rusty would have seen Annalee with her left hand outstretched, gazing at Brad's heirloom engagement ring and wedding band.

Later that night Annalee placed those love tokens in a kitchen drawer where she kept outdated coupons, notes from her mother, paper clips, a flashlight and a compass.

Chapter 11

The Leap

Annalee returned from the travel agency, posted her flight itinerary on her bulletin board—San Francisco to Seattle, to Anchorage, to Fairbanks and return in ten days—and glided upstairs. In her parents' tiled bathroom with its skylight and chrome fixtures she drew a full 50 gallons of water onto lavender bath oil, bath salts, bath milk and bath foam. And then she stood with one foot suspended over the lip of the tub.

Whose foot is this, she asked aloud. Surely not mine. My foot never had those ropey sinews and, dear Lord, a tuft of hair in the center of each big toe. Whose blue veins are these? Whose thigh sagging just enough to show the start of that crepe-like skin? After their first conversation Rusty never again outraged her with sexualized innuendoes but the path they were taking clearly led to intimacy. No one had looked at her bare limbs since Brad and he hadn't often glanced her way by the end of their marriage. Her body had become a foreign territory, not traversed even by herself. Now a man would be looking. And judging.

Annalee sunk below the bubbles. She didn't want to evaluate the texture of her skin, its color—that pale cast, she might be an Alaskan Native herself, flailing away at a bone carving in a land where the sun seldom shines between October and March. She lifted her calf, scooping the bubbles away with her palm. How long had it been since she had shaved her legs? Or worn makeup, had a manicure? With only days remaining until her journey it was too late to correct the sags and sinews but she could use a speedy upgrade for the rest. Hair, nails, makeup, the works. But where to go?

Until Brad left her for a beautician at Classic Trends, the beauty parlor across the street from his garage, Annalee would visit that salon every six weeks to have her distinctive auburn hair shaped and styled by Bella, a casual acquaintance since high school. After the breakup Classic Trends seemed like a mine field. Bella surely must have known about the affair between Annalee's husband and Aura who no doubt had been traipsing back and forth in full view of the other beauticians and their customers, returning to her station with her tiny tie-dyed clothing awry and her braids in an uproar. And Annalee knew that the San Amaro rumor engine would roar into overdrive if she crossed the threshold to Classic Trends. She imagined a crowd forming before the storefront window, anticipating a cat fight with her and Aura rolling on the floor amid the hair trimmings. She was reluctant to visit the town's only other beauty salon, Bonnie's Hair And Nail. It was hunkered down in a modular home on the outskirts of town, shared space with a dog groomer and had a questionable reputation. So, in the years since the breakup Annalee had learned to cut her own hair. The result was good enough for a woman who seldom ventured beyond her daily rounds at H.A.G.L. and Vera's Market.

"What do you do about your eyebrows?" Annalee asked T'Angeline the next day in the staff lounge.

"What do I do *what* about my eyebrows?" T'Angeline furrowed her perfectly-shaped brows.

"You know, who tweezes them for you so they're fat where they meet in the middle and taper off at the ends?"

"What?" T'Angeline's eyes widened. "My eyebrows are fat and they meet in the middle?"

"No, no, T'Angeline. Your eyebrows aren't fat. Let's start over. Would you like a Diet Pepsi?"

"That does it, Annalee. I don't give a flying fuck if she's pregnant with your ex's Siamese triplets. I've been putting up long enough with these chicken shit beauticians at Bonnie's Hair and Nail. Bonnie takes them right out of beauty school because they're cheaper that way and most of them should have flunked. I could have been going to Aura at Classic Trends but did I betray you? I did not!"

Annalee groaned inwardly. Did her so-called personal life dictate even the choice of beauty salons among her casual acquaintances? T'Angeline went on.

"Aura is totally up to speed on the music scene chicks. She can do hair and makeup like all the big stars, everyone from Stevie Nicks to Siouxsie Sioux. But us ladies at H.A.G.L., do we get to look cool? Noooo. It's 'oh, we can't go to Classic Trends. Oh, Annalee would be upset. Oh, we'll all go to Bonnie and come out looking like we stuck our heads in a garbage disposal.' "

Annalee shook her own head to clear unpleasant visual images of garbage disposal mayhem. "T'An, honey, you look beautiful all the time but if you want to see Aura you go right ahead. I won't care, even if you come out looking like Siouxsie Sioux."

Thus, Annalee made another choice for change. There would be no time to recover if a visit to Bonnie's resulted in disaster. With no further options the alternative was an upscale salon in Gold Park, a bedroom community 20 miles away where there was an opening for Annalee that afternoon.

The beautician, Donna, appeared to be about Annalee's age which was an optimistic start. She didn't trust her hair to one of the post-adolescents at the other stations. Some appeared to be painting their customers' hair with brushes dipped in neon-colored Jell-O.

"Wonderful hair," Donna said, plunging her hands into Annalee's curls and lifting them. She met Annalee's eyes in the mirror and smiled. "Great body and shine. The ends are very dry, though. Let's start by taking off just the dead parts, only a few inches. Then we'll layer it for thickness, give it a good conditioning and next time you come back we can try some highlights if you'd like, deepen the richness of the red. Let's try a whole new look. A new look for a new decade?"

As Donna outlined the transformation Annalee felt increasing discomfort. Her bathtub epiphany had failed to consider a crucial detail. Loss of freedom. Until she gave up on love, she had been part of the vast population of women and even some men who invested time, money and effort to beauty and to thwarting the signs of age. She had moisturized, exfoliated, shaved, plucked, soaked and buffed. Every Monday, Wednesday and Friday she would spend a miserable hour in an aerobics class attempting to mimic the movements of a woman half her age who wore a Spandex body suit and cried, "c'mon ladies, work those abs, work those glutes, feel those quadriceps burn!" After Brad left she didn't care if her arms jiggled, if her T-spot was oily and her ends were split. Yet, sensible diet and the physical demands of her job helped her maintain a satisfying level of fitness. Her bare skin was clean and clear, nails neatly shaped on Sundays while she watched the news on TV. She hadn't been a slave to the dictates of *Vogue* and *Cosmopolitan* for years. Until this moment she hadn't realized that she enjoyed the liberation.

With Annalee's continued silence Donna eventually stopped talking and rested her hand on Annalee's shoulder. "So," she said. Annalee appeared now to be gazing into her own eyes in the mirror. A moment passed.

"So," Annalee replied at last. Then she reached into her purse and withdrew $20. She handed it to Donna. "Thanks anyway." The beautician's brow furrowed and she was still gazing down at the money in her hand as if it were a foreign object as Annalee walked away.

At the Gold Park mall Annalee spent the remainder of her upgrade budget at Sports And Fitness. She came away with sturdy thermal underwear and Arctic hiking books. When she returned home, as a concession she shaved her legs and, as an afterthought, the center of each big toe.

⌒

Annalee kept her guilty secret until it was nearly too late. When the moment of truth arrived it was more painful than she could ever have feared.

"I'm about to go nuts, Annalee," Ivy said over the phone on the evening before Annalee's departure. "Between Mike's parents coming for Thanksgiving and this insane Halloween costume party at H.A.G.L. tomorrow I swear I'm going to become a Muslim. Wait. Do Muslims celebrate Halloween and Thanksgiving?"

"I don't know. Look, Ivy . . . ."

"We need to sit Marvin down and have a talk about the H.A.G.L. social scene. I know he adores us and wants us to love him but he's going about it the wrong way. Plus I nearly shit last year when T'Angeline showed up as a unicorn with that big dick-like thing sticking out of her forehead. I'm scared to think what she'll inflict on us this time. What are you going as?"

It was time. Annalee drew a breath. "I'm not going."

"Well . . . wow. Atta girl! Stick up for yourself! Me, I can't stand to see Marvin looking all puppy-eyed. Come on over afterwards and we'll take the kids trick-or-treating."

"Ivy, I won't be here tomorrow. I'm leaving for a few days."

"Oh? Going to Vegas? Your dad's not sick again, is he?"

"No, Ivy. I'm going to Alaska." Only silence came across the telephone line. "Ivy?"

"You're going to Alaska." It was more a statement than a question. "And you're going tomorrow. What the fuck, Annalee."

"Please don't be mad."

"I just saw you yesterday! You never said a thing about it. So what other secrets do you have? I assume this is about Sheepskin Man. Have you two opened a blubber restaurant in Chakinakimakinak? Or no, let's be reasonable. Are you pregnant?"

"Ivy, you're over-reacting."

"Over-reacting? Bullshit. I've seen this coming for months. Ever since that cartoon showed up in March you've been slipping farther and farther away. People talk to you and you look like you can't remember who we are. Now you tell me you're going thousands of miles north to see a man I assume you don't know. Or maybe you've been sneaking up there on your days off. What the hell is this about? I thought we were friends."

"Look, Ivy." Annalee paused. "I don't know how to say this, so I'll just say it. I feel like you and Mom and just about everyone in San Amaro have this agenda for me. I have to be in a relationship, I'm nothing without a man, I need help, it's your job to help me, blah, blah, blah. It's like I'm some Peace Corps project." Annalee heard Ivy gasp but she pressed on. "I told you when he first showed up, I started this thing with the guy in Alaska as a joke. But I've been talking to him. There's something about Alaska. It makes me feel like my blood's been frozen in my veins but now it's flowing again. Do you understand?"

"No. Do you?"

"Part of me wanted to tell you all along. But Ivy, I knew once I did that, everyone in town would find out. I just wanted to have a piece of my own life for a change."

"I don't believe this. You concocted a secret life because I talk about you? I talk about you, Annalee, because I care about you. I feel as if . . . as if I need help dealing with you because you won't deal with yourself."

"Maybe you should just stop trying to 'deal' with me! Try being a friend instead."

The line went dead.

Annalee knew her parents' routine. Every Tuesday night at 8 they picked up some neighbors and went to The Strip. Mrs. Krasney would hit the slots while the others saw a show at The Tropicana. Annalee waited until 9 p.m. to call their answering machine. She left her parents a voicemail that said she was taking a long-overdue vacation, she was going to Alaska, would return in ten days, and would call as soon as she returned. She knew they would also find a message from Ivy.

There was one more call to make before she unplugged her telephone. Although Marvin gave everyone his home phone number for emergencies, thoughts about improving the ambience at H.A.G.L. and the occasional dinner invitation, she called the machine on his desk. When he arrived in the morning he heard a soothing, reassuring message from an employee whose absence could send his blood pressure into the stratosphere. And he found the careful list of instructions that Annalee had placed neatly in the center of The Island Of All Returns.

PART TWO:

ALASKA, 1990

Chapter 12

The Goods Are Odd

  Annalee caught her reflection in the wide plate glass window outside San Francisco International Airport. She saw a woman in Arctic boots, an open ski parka and hood with a ruff of faux fur over a black silk blouse circa 1942 over a turtleneck sweater, insulated gloves stuffed into a side pocket. Levi's from an infamous photograph, chenille scarf that trailed to her knees, an aviator cap and hoop earrings. Then she strode to the Alaska Airlines gate carrying a scuffed Navy-issue duffle bag in which were her new thermal underwear, sturdy outerwear, three tubes of ChapStick, basic hygiene products in the event they didn't have toothpaste and shampoo in Alaska, and a cobalt blue silk nightgown and robe. Other than her new underwear and hiking boots from the shopping spree at Gold Park, most of her attire came from Evelyn's trove in the attic with some items from a hasty outing to the Salvation Army that morning. Those items included the duffle bag. She wouldn't go to Alaska pulling a suitcase on wheels as if she were the district attorney.

  The itinerary took her to Seattle for a brief layover, then she faced the long flight north above the western seaboard across Canada. She dozed and read and gazed at the cloudy sky below and eventually found herself decanted into the tiny Anchorage airport. Only 15 minutes separated her from the connecting flight into the Alaskan interior.

  It was a small jet, an 80-seat Q400 Bombardier, straddling a yellow line out on the tarmac that took Annalee and 30 other travelers north to Fairbanks. As they boarded she glanced at the other passengers and counted only five other women of whom three appeared to be Native with long black hair nearly to their waists. Once airborne Annalee looked down at Anchorage, a town no larger than San Amaro, and realized this was the largest urban metropolis in a state the size of New

England and Texas combined. She listened to the conversations around her.

"I been fishing 33 years now, never stopped, not even for Veterans Day."

"They don't let you bring your dog even if you buy it a ticket in first class."

"We're catching the bush plane out of Ruby this evening, take the kids trick-or-treating down to Fairbanks. We'll be stuck there till they head back on Friday but the kids don't mind missing school."

"We got a moose up around Talkeetna but the wind stopped so we had to sit on it and row all the way back down river."

Below, the mountainous landscape flattened and the palette of green and blue shifted to white, shades of black, cream and gray. The tracks of tributaries branched away from a river. Deep woods filled crevasses. The plane pitched and yawed. Granite and snow, shadow and sunlight, Annalee watched the geographic features sharpen and define as the aircraft began its descent. The passengers stood and several fished in the overhead bins. As she monitored the unfamiliar landscape below Annalee felt inexplicably as if she were coming home from exile. Her breath caught in her throat.

The captain's intercom switched on. "Ladies and gentlemen, we are now approaching the Denali Range. Those of you who are standing will have a clear view of the 'fasten seat belt' sign which is clearly lit over your heads," he quipped. At any other time Annalee would have appreciated the sarcasm. Instead she wept with longing, then wiped her eyes as the plane bumped to a halt. The doors opened to a heavy sky and a terminal smaller than H.A.G.L. Snow covered the ground in a thin layer.

The air was fiercely cold, sharp and clean and she followed the other passengers onto the tarmac. The rest of the field was filled with two-seater aircraft in a variety of colors and states of air-worthiness. Some seemed to have wings made of canvas. Others were muddy, scraped and scarred. Annalee wanted to approach and touch each one, climb into cabins, hear the small engines come to life. She shook her head and followed the crowd.

The tiny terminal lobby was dwarfed by a stuffed polar bear. He stood on hind legs with his head rising 20 feet above a single row of seats. Even in a glass case his eyes appeared to monitor Annalee's progress toward the small baggage conveyor belt. No one spoke her name. She applied a coat of ChapStick and watched as suitcases, skis, backpacks and what appeared to be a rifle in a hand-made leather case came down the belt, then finally her duffle bag with one side open and a sweater spilling out. She snagged it and then, after all of the moments of speculation, was straddling it on the floor with her hair awry, pounding on the snaps, when she glanced up to see muddy boots and, above them, blue jeans and the bottom edge of that jacket.

 She had planned to hug him gently, thank him for his hospitality, set a tone of warmth coupled with polite distance. Instead, to her own surprise she flung herself into his arms. He smelled of engine oil and wood smoke and the jacket was smooth under her palms. He grinned at her, picked up her bag, took her hand and wordlessly drew her beside him. Outside at the curb with its engine idling was a mud-spattered vehicle the size of a UPS delivery truck. Its headlights were covered in wire mesh. Rusty opened the side door for Annalee. She saw that the interior was lined with wooden shelves on which jars were bolted down and filled with nuts, bolts and washers. A machine the size of a ride-on lawn mower was strapped to the floor with canvas belts and beside it were rags, tools, rope, poles, pipes, something that appeared to be an airplane propeller and dozens of paper coffee cups. She pushed aside a coil of rubber tubing on the passenger seat and gingerly slid in. Rusty took the wheel, put his right hand on her knee, pressed it gently and they pulled out onto the road.

 "Trip OK?" he asked.

 "It was . . . ." She reached for words to describe the flight north and her emotions as the aircraft descended, then held back. "Yes, it was."

 Around them the landscape was flat with hills in the distance and dark trees lining the two-lane road. Annalee saw no homes and few other vehicles. They rode in silence, which Annalee found comforting. She merely wanted to absorb the paradoxical feeling of rawness and familiarity.

 They drove in comfortable silence for nearly an hour. Just as the sun was disappearing below the horizon she noticed in the distance a battered jeep. It approached, slowed, Rusty slowed, and both pulled over to the shoulder and stopped. A man in camouflage gear hopped out of the jeep and walked over.

"Hey," he said. His eyes slid over to Annalee and back to Rusty. "You seen Rick?"

"Naw."

The men gazed up into the darkening sky. A moment passed.

"You go out with Drew to that hunt at Nowitna?" Rusty asked.

"Yeah, I'm heading back tomorrow. Drew brought tarps for the moose."

"Oh, pop a moose did they?"

Pop. Annalee marked the casual description of aiming, firing and bringing down a creature the size of a horse.

"Yeah. It's a guy from Montana and his son. Kid was so excited he nearly peed. I guess they been planning this shoot since the kid was born. They're still up there camped out so they can finish packing the meat."

Rusty grinned. "Guess we're gonna be hearing complaints about blood on the floor of that plane again. I told Drew he should get his own Piper, let his old lady fly hers whenever she needs, go shopping for makeup."

"Yeah, then she can just bleed on it herself."

Annalee cringed as the men guffawed. Neither acknowledged her.

Finally Rusty said, "Kenny, this-here's Annalee from California. Annalee, this is my little brother Kenny."

Clearly the long desolate road from Fairbanks to Garnet was a place where one could recognize a vehicle from a quarter mile away and it would be driven by one's brother and no one would be surprised.

The two men leaned against the truck and continued to talk about work and weather and if Milo would get the trench dug before the ground froze solid.

After Kenny left Rusty said, "bet he looked familiar, huh?"

"I can see a family resemblance."

"I mean, from *Alaskan Bachelors?* He was in there too, three pages ahead of me. I thought you'd notice that we had the same last name."

Annalee had looked at nothing other than each man's age. Kenny was probably in his late 30s and one of the last supplicants in the issue to meet his fate in The Ollie Machine.

◦

After a rutted path through dense woods they reached a clearing Annalee had come to know from Rusty's pictures. He parked before his cabin. In the twilight of an Alaskan afternoon on the last day in October, the structure appeared to loom. A light shining through one window saved it from seeming foreboding.

"Let's take a look at Blue Lady," Rusty murmured. He helped her out of the truck with one arm around her waist and guided her to a small landing strip behind the cabin. A fuel pump with a sign reading "Av-gas" stood on a flat spot some distance away and a single airplane wing rested against a small shed. In the near distance Annalee saw the airplane. It seemed minuscule.

"Is this it? I mean, her?" Were airplanes female or was that only boats?

"Yup, this is her. Piper SuperCub, best friend a bush pilot ever had. I can land her on a beach, sling her tail over my shoulder and pull her along anywhere I want to go."

When they reached the craft Rusty leaned against it. "Sometimes," he said, "when the fishing season is on, I can spend more than eight hours a day in this cockpit. Blue Lady's my office, kitchen table, den, entertainment center, sometimes from sunup to sundown I just land to pee and refuel." Annalee tried to imagine spending a full working day thousands of feet above the sea in an area the size of a roller coaster seat at the county fair. "Thank heavens she's never been my bedroom," he continued. "The day I fall asleep at the controls is the day I know I'm too old to do this work."

"She's a beauty," Annalee said although she didn't know if Blue Lady was a beauty or a wreck. She stepped close enough to touch the propeller, moved it experimentally to show she was interested. Rusty's expression became concerned.

"Best not to touch," he said. "That way, if something goes wrong I'll know it's my fault."

She noticed that the small craft rested on two large soft-looking tires without treads. Their surfaces were smooth and shining. The cockpit was covered by a clear dome and through it she could see an array of dials and switches. Blue Lady didn't appear sturdy enough to survive a breeze, much less the punishment it must endure over the open ocean. Rusty patted the airplane's side, then hefted Annalee's duffle bag and she preceded him wordlessly to the cabin where they crossed a rough-hewn porch.

The eyes met hers when she stepped across the threshold. Row upon row of eyes in dozens of animal heads mounted on every wall. All eyes were shining, fixed, all pupils large and round like the eyes of cocaine addicts. Annalee gasped. Facing her was the skull of a massive creature. Unlike the other heads this one was bare of hide. Its hollow eye sockets looked out above a set of gleaming tusks that appeared to be three feet in length. "Mother of God!" Annalee cried, involuntarily stepping back and colliding with Rusty behind her. Tusks, she thought frantically. But clearly not those of an elephant. Tusks but not an elephant. An elephant seal? The animal must have been impossibly huge.

"What is that creature?" she asked weakly.

"Bull walrus," Rusty said casually as he ushered her through the door. "Found the carcass on the beach out on Wrangel Island six years ago. He's an old guy and he was pretty beat up, blood everywhere, gashes a foot deep, probably done in by a young stud who wanted his harem. They don't usually kill each other but it happens." Rusty leaned her duffle bag against the wall. "Only Natives can hunt them but us other folks can take them if they're dead already." He pulled off his boots as he spoke. "I was so excited, I came on home and flew back with my chainsaw. Two thousand miles round trip praying all the way that nobody would get to him before I did. Cost me three months' pay in aviation fuel but it was worth it. This fellow is choice." Annalee, following Rusty's lead, removed her shoes without taking her eyes from those of the beast. "Cut the head off and flew it back here. My neighbor Andy is a hunter and a taxidermist, been here most of his life. He's had his hands on just about everything and says these are the best tusks he ever saw."

Annalee watched a mental movie of Rusty flying across the tundra in frail Blue Lady with an oozing, tusk-bearing head on the passenger seat. Shoes off now and looking around, she counted 15 more heads. Most sported antlers, matching snouts, ears, hides covered with varying lengths and textures of fur or hair. She stepped slightly to the left and, like those of the polar bear at the airport, the glassy eyes seemed to mark her movement.

"Got that elk up at Akiachak two years ago."

Which one was the elk? Several heads were large with small antlers, others were small with large antlers. Were they antlers or horns? Disoriented, Annalee tore her eyes from those in the heads and looked around. She had more vital concerns than to convince Rusty she could not at that moment have distinguished an elk from a brontosaurus.

The door to what could have been a saloon, painted blue, was balanced horizontally across four file cabinets and evidently served as a dining room table. On it were papers, a weapon that could have been a rifle or shotgun, and a large object that rested beside a jar of bolts. From her life as a hardware store employee Annalee recognized the object as a torque wrench, a tool typically used in engine repair. Attempting to behave as if a torque wrench was a reasonable object to find on a dining room table, Annalee offered, "looks like a torque wrench. Were you working on your van?" Rusty peeled off his jacket and hung it on a hook.

"Nope. Had to take a mule apart yesterday," she heard him say.

Did these people spend their lives up to their knees in animal carcasses? She glanced around to see if she could spot a mule head on the wall. "I wonder why you'd want to take apart a barnyard animal when you have all these wild ones? And wouldn't you use a knife?"

"Oh, sorry. I forget we speak our own language. It's M.A.U.L.E.," he spelled. "You pronounce it 'mule.' It's an airplane. Andy next door has one. She's got some sort of weird vibration, started after he wrecked her up by Barrow six years ago. Let me show you around."

Annalee's head was spinning but she stood and followed Rusty through the dining room and a living room/gym with weights and a stationary bicycle. He stopped at a closed door.

"This is your bathroom," he said and turned the doorknob.

"I have my own bathroom?"

"Sure. Girls don't like to share the john with boys, do they?" Rusty stepped aside.

A potpourri of roses, Patchouli oil and L'Air du Temps perfume wafted surreally out into the hall. Annalee, anticipating more disembodied heads, at first was unable to make sense of what she saw and smelled. Lining the shelves, the toilet tank and counter top were pink towels, bars of pink soap, bottles with labels that listed shampoo, bubble bath, conditioner and hand lotion. Pink washcloth, brush and comb, pink candles, rose-hued mats on the floor, new toothbrush still in its wrapper, mouthwash, a floral shower curtain and a bathroom scale. This "john" could have been teleported in from a seraglio. Rusty turned and continued down the hall with Annalee, rendered speechless by cognitive dissonance, silently following. They reached the bedroom, in the center of which was a king-sized bed. Rusty sat on the edge and met her eyes.

"So, Annalee, here we are."

"What? Oh, right. Here we are." Still in disbelief Annalee looked over her shoulder toward the bathroom.

"And look. We've both had relationships," he said.

"Uh . . . OK." She decided this wasn't the moment to remind him that she'd been alone for five years and before that she'd married right out of high school. They had covered their relationship histories months ago and had broached the subject of sex. After nearly a year of conversation, they would cross the bridge to intimacy when the time was right. It was foolish and unnecessary to feign coyness.

"What I'm getting at," Rusty continued, "is you can sleep in the spare bedroom if you want. Or you can sleep in this bed and I can sleep in the spare bedroom. I can take you back to town to the motel in Garnet. Or you can sleep with me." His voice was matter-of-fact and he continued to hold her eyes.

"I'd like to sleep with you," she said simply.

"All right then." He stood and took her hand. "Let's go fix dinner. I thought you'd like to try some authentic Alaskan king crab."

Chapter 13

Female Presence

After their meal was finished they stayed at the table for an hour sipping the fragrant Zinfandel that Annalee had brought from home, and telling stories of their lives, some for the second time. During their months of conversation Annalee had told Rusty anecdotes about Marvin, Ivy, T'Angeline and the H.A.G.L. crew but their antics came alive when the stories were retold in person. Rusty described his childhood in the south and life in Alaska before "all the Yuppies started trying to turn the Last Frontier into L.A." Finally he walked around the table, tilted her chin up, kissed her gently on the lips and said, "well, time to hit the rack. I'm going to wash up. You need anything?"

Annalee couldn't imagine what might have been left out of that bathroom except a maid servant to squeeze the toothpaste tube.

She took her time preparing for bed. And then flossed, brushed, showered, face creamed and hair fluffed she realized that her cobalt silk nightgown was in her duffle bag in Rusty's bedroom and the clothes in which she had traveled since morning were lying in a moist heap at her feet. Ultimately nothing remained but to wrap herself in a towel and pad down the hallway in her bare feet. She could slip into her nightgown under cover of darkness. Hoping Rusty had turned out the lights, she approached the bedroom. She found him reading an airplane magazine, sitting up in bed with glasses on and wet comb tracks in his hair. He glanced up at her. "I was going to warm your side for you but it's not all that cold." He turned to put his book on the nightstand while Annalee sidled to the far side of the bed and realized she had no way to retrieve her nightgown without an obvious juggling act. Mercifully, Rusty doused the light and Annalee came to bed wearing a damp towel.

He didn't touch her. They lay side by side, Rusty breathing evenly. Annalee was surprised and grateful for his willingness to take things slow. It spoke to care and sensitivity. He had probably been deprived of sex here in the isolated wilderness.

"I need to keep these heavy shades over the windows," he said after a moment, "because the sun stays up all night long in the summer. Makes you crazy." She could hear the smile in his voice. "By the time winter comes I'm too lazy to drag them all down again. Are you comfortable?"

"Mm hmm."

Two minutes passed in silence. Finally Annalee turned and placed her palm over his heart. His skin was warm. He slipped an arm under her head. That was all. Another minute passed. She could see from the dim light in the hallway that his eyes were open. She lightly caressed his chest. He stroked her shoulder. She ran her hand gently along his side. He touched her breast and then moved his hand to her waist and gently turned her body toward him. Each time she took intimacy one step deeper he followed, never making the first move. It was another 15 minutes before they were having sex. Annalee felt that she would faint with desire.

And then, while most of her awareness gave over entirely to the experience, a small increment of attention was alert and puzzled. Although Annalee had little prior experience to serve as comparison, there was no mistaking this Alaskan bachelor's skill as a sexual partner. He knew every zone, what it did, when to start and stop. He knew how to read her, to listen to her breath, what to do when she sighed or moaned. He knew positions without being athletic or competitive, how to give and take so that when she responded to his response he would deepen it, his breath catching in his throat, urging her on without demanding.

The rugged nature of his cabin spoke to the absence of feminine influence . . . except, of course, for the bathroom. And that was not the work of a woman unless the woman believed that rose, Patchouli oil and L'Air du Temps were a seductive olfactory combination. Likewise, the visual avalanche of pink objects seemed to be the work, not of a woman but of a man who wanted to impress a woman. Or women.

Ultimately desire overcame thought and she lost herself in Rusty's perfection.

When she opened her eyes again the clock on his bedside table showed that another 45 minutes had passed. She had climaxed twice, both orgasms shaking the bed and sending a cascade of fine shivers along her body. His followed. When they were still, he reached down to the floor and lifted a square of sheepskin to place under her hips.

"I thought we were going to tear the bed apart," he whispered.

"I think I lost consciousness." After a few more breaths she rose on one elbow to prepare for the journey down the hall to shower.

"No, stay here with me," Rusty said. "Just another minute more. I want to enjoy the experience of being together."

It was the suggestion of a man who was practiced at seduction. It wasn't the sort of practice one did alone.

⁓

Annalee was sitting up in bed with her arms around her knees, looking out at the bare branches of trees shadowing the barn, when she felt Rusty stir beside her. His palm caressed her calf.

"Hi, baby. You're sure looking good to me."

Annalee stretched and turned so that her body was touching his. "Mm, you are too. Can we go outside?"

"Can we go out *now*?"

"Well, no, not right now . . . ."

Later, dressed and drinking coffee at the table, Annalee was caught again when Rusty saw her musing through the kitchen window.

"OK, let's go out before you bust a gut. Come here." Rusty led her to a closet door. "All my sisters and daughters have been here, and you don't need stuff like this where they live. They leave it behind. There's a ton of it. You're about the same size as my sister Sheena Kay." Annalee briefly wondered what sort of mother would name a child Sheena Kay. Rusty peered over at a thermometer mounted on the outside window. "It's ten degrees out there right now. That teeny little jacket and those skimpy gloves aren't going to do you any good." Annalee said a mental farewell to what she thought was adequate preparation for Alaska on the first day of November. "You can wear anything you want."

Annalee saw women's overalls, jackets, gloves, boots, sweaters and socks in every size and color. Rusty's sisters and daughters must have bought out all the military surplus and sporting goods stores in the deep south. Or were the former owners really members of his family? Again the thought nibbled at the edges of her awareness and she watched a brief mental image of women rushing from the cabin, jettisoning their Arctic gear in their wakes. She sifted through the clothing and chose a soft woolen turtleneck sweater, a thermal vest, some leggings, a pair of overalls. As she layered, she tucked cuffs into socks and sleeves, turned edges under to thwart drafts and finished with thermal gloves.

"I thought you had never been in cold country," Rusty commented. "Given the right stuff to choose from you dress like a pro."

"I'm just putting on what makes sense."

"Well, you have good instincts, Annalee. People need that to survive here." He pulled on a pair of canvas Carhartt overalls and opened the front door.

Annalee stepped out into flinty air so cold that it stung her throat on the first inhale. Now more alert to her surroundings than the evening before, she smelled snow, ice, wood, fur, mud, mountains and water.

"Let's head down to the river." With his arm around her Rusty guided her into the woods. Their boots crunched on a new layer of snow that had fallen in the night. Annalee noted birch trees, fallen logs, and she heard geese overhead. The sky seemed vast and thick with lumbering black-bottomed clouds. At the path's end was a wide ice-covered river and on the opposite bank, a thick dark forest. Annalee looked across the water. The woods were still and silent with bare, blackened branches reaching up to the sky.

As she stood motionless she felt a presence. Its immediacy was profound and she involuntarily glanced over her shoulder, expecting to find that she was being watched. She saw only Rusty, beside her, looking into the trees. She slowed her breath, curled her fingers into fists in her pockets and planted her feet more firmly on the snow. The presence became more pronounced. The landscape seemed to have become sentient. And its overriding quality was indifference. Annalee marked that sense above all. It was neither benevolent nor hostile. It seemed female, dark and covert, judging her but without passion.

Then the incongruous sound of a telephone rang through the silence.

"I need to get that, Rusty said. "It might be about work. There's nothing dangerous out here. But don't wander off." He trotted away toward the cabin.

Annalee felt nearly reluctant to face the woods alone, but steeled herself. When she did, the sensation she had noted was gone. It's only woods, she reminded herself. There is nothing out there. And then, as if it had never dissipated, it returned. She wanted to surrender to it, but not as she had given in to the excitement and unfamiliarity of Rusty the night before. With him, for all of the drama and intrigue, Annalee felt self contained. She might get lost in the relationship for a time but she would come back to herself. This emotion, in contrast, portended something darker, more compelling, nearly hypnotic. Then the presence seemed again to turn its attention elsewhere, dismissing her. Overhead the clouds appeared to have separate lives, lumbering and towering. The ice-covered river became steely with the glare momentarily tempered by overcast. Annalee felt a curious sense of abandonment.

She heard the sound of Rusty's boots as he made his way back down the path. "A neighbor of mine is in trouble," he said. "Her, ah, her husband fell off the roof and might have broken his ankle. She can't get her car started. I'm going to head over and take them into Fairbanks. Are you going to be OK here until I get back?"

Apparently Annalee wasn't invited. "I'll be fine."

They hurried back to the cabin. "I wish I had time to start another fire for you but I need to rush. A fireplace is a bitch if you've never dealt with one before." They came inside and Rusty took his keys from a hook by the door. "There's a space heater you can plug in if you feel chilly but the place is still warm from the fire this morning. Sure you're OK?"

Annalee nodded and he kissed her and left. In a moment she heard the sound of his van's engine, starting and then growing distant.

Alone, Annalee was better able to take in Rusty's life. A row of heavy jackets hung from pegs sunk into the wall and piles of maps were stacked along the baseboards. On one wall a huge aerial map of Alaska was disfigured by notes, tacks, penned-in cryptic numbers and post-its. Other than the animal heads, Rusty's décor consisted of framed photos of airplanes. There was, Annalee noticed again, no sign of a woman's presence. She opened the refrigerator. Rusty had stocked it with fresh fruit and vegetables, containers of yogurt, crab legs, several steaks and a case of beer.

She wandered to the fireplace and stood gazing down into the remains of a previous blaze. Coaxing the fire back to life wouldn't be that difficult. Humans had been making fire for millennia. Granted it had taken centuries for them to control it but this fireplace appeared to be well-made. Relying on memory of movies and novels, she stirred the embers and over them laid a flat bed of kindling with two trips to the entryway for twigs. On top of that she placed newspaper, then several branches. She experimented with the smoke, the flue, the air flow. When Rusty returned some two hours later it was to a warmed living room, a fire crackling in the hearth and Annalee asleep before it with her jacket draped over her shoulders.

The next day Annalee offered to make her special San Francisco-style crab cioppino. Alaskan king crab would be even more succulent than the variety available in San Amaro and she'd need only a few more ingredients from the tiny grocery store which also served as a gas station and post office in Garnet.

Rusty left for the groceries, calling over his shoulder, "Is it OK to invite Kenny and his girlfriend Katie? They're homesteading a quarter mile down the river."

So evidently Kenny had met someone through *Alaskan Bachelors* too. And they were living together. It would be good to share this experience with another woman.

"Sure. Just double everything on the list and there'll be plenty to go around."

Kenny's girlfriend Katie was a chubby, apple-cheeked blonde and she seemed nearly obsessively devoted to Kenny and to demonstrating that they were a couple. When she spoke, which was seldom, her few anecdotes were of fishing with Kenny, hunting with Kenny and cooking for Kenny. She rarely left his side.

Annalee was curious about her. If Katie had met Rusty's brother through his *Alaskan Bachelors* profile last December she almost certainly was not from Alaska. She must come from an environment where she had previously learned to shoot and skin a caribou . . . not skills a woman typically learns at all, much less in the span of less than a year. And if she had not opted to go gill fishing with Kenny, where evidently she had needed to stand up in a boat and keep water from spilling into her hip waders and drowning her, would Kenny abandon her? Annalee became even more curious after dinner when the four went for a hike along the riverbank. The women shyly chatted while the men walked ahead.

"Five years ago," Katie said, "me and Kenny went back to Georgia to meet his family. I swear that place was crawling with snakes. And bugs? I've seen kindergarten children smaller than some of them damned things."

Five years ago? After the couple went home Annalee asked Rusty about this curiosity.

"Oh, that's just Kenny. He and Katie have been together since he moved up here eight years ago. He doesn't have the nerve to break up with her but he wanted to try something different. In fact he was the one who found out about *Alaskan Bachelors* and talked me into it."

"He was involved with Katie when he advertised himself as a single available man throughout the United States and beyond? That's heinous. Did she find out?"

"I think she answered the phone one time and there were these two ladies from Alabama . . . ." Rusty shook his head and laughed. "Kenny had a lot of explaining to do. Poor bastard."

So this explained Katie's insecure clinging. Annalee took a dim view of Kenny's behavior. And she was troubled by Rusty's casual, permissive attitude.

By the next afternoon, steeped in Alaska, Annalee felt that she had entered an altered state. She would rise from the table and dreamily walk out into the woods. There, she would reach down into the snow, pick up those fragments of wood that the beavers would leave behind in their industrious felling of the trees, turn them over in her hands and come back to the cabin with pockets full as if she had been beach combing on some strange shore. Rusty took her to see the glaciers at Denali State Park. From photos and documentaries she recognized the changes in hue and texture. She knew that more lay below the surface and that each glacier might hold artifacts so ancient and yet so perfectly preserved that the mastodon's eye might seem ready to wink. Their blue was the color of cold itself, more cold than anything white. But in their presence she sensed that no media can communicate one spellbinding quality of glaciers. Like Alaska itself but in a more subtle way, they seemed to be alive.

She plied Rusty for information. She craved knowledge of the environment, how to read the sky, smell the air, know where ice was thick and thin. Win its approval.

"Would you teach me how to shoot that gun on the table?"

"No."

"Why not?"

"Because you've never handled a firearm. Right?" He waited for her nod. "I don't want to make another trip to the hospital this week. That thing has a mean kick. It can break your trigger finger and bruise your shoulder. I have to say, though, you're dealing with Alaska better than any of the other ladies who . . . ." He stopped, wide-eyed.

"Than any of the other ladies who," she prompted.

"But look, maybe next time you're here I'll get a little Winchester .22 pump-action rifle and teach you how to fire it, OK? You're really good at Alaska, Annalee." His words were hasty and pressured. Annalee sensed that he was backfilling over his gaffe. "I saw you carry your boots in from the mud room. That shows good thinking. Some people would leave them by the door and then freeze their feet off next time they put them on but you knew better. And you turned your hood under when you took it off outside so it won't collect snow that you'd dump on your head when you put it back on. It's like you've been here all your life . . . ."

At some point before she left Annalee would ask him how many "other ladies" had preceded her and why they were apparently no longer in his life.

Chapter 14

All Over the Place

On her sixth morning in Alaska Annalee and Rusty made love and when they were silent he asked what she was thinking.

"I'm thinking that I'm scattered all over the place," she said with a laugh. "I'm sure I left eyeliner in the bathroom, I'm ashamed to say. And there's a certain pair of underpants I can't quite locate. I've left tracks in the snow and I suspect the beavers are feeling miffed about it. I don't know how I'm going to pack up when I leave on Sunday."

"Yes," he said quietly. "You are scattered all over the place. You're on the porch watching the snow, in my study room looking at my books, out at the river, in bed with me driving me half crazy. You are, Annalee. You're scattered all over the place and I don't know how I can just watch you pack up and leave."

"Whoa. I did not see this coming."

"Where do I stand with you, Annalee? I want to know. Do you want to move to Alaska some day? Is this just a fling? Am I like visiting some alien from another planet?"

"Rusty, I honestly haven't thought about it. I'm having a great time here. And there's something about Alaska. I can't pin it down. It calls to me. But you and I are so different from each other and I haven't been in a relationship for a long time. I can't think about living here so soon. Are you talking about a long-term commitment? If I were here I'd need to be dependent on you. I hardly know you yet. I've never made impulsive decisions and that one could lead to disaster or, at the very least, hurt feelings."

"Then let's see how things go, OK? I won't pressure you. But will you keep an open mind about me? It's just . . . I've never seen a woman take to this place like you." Again this didn't seem to be the moment to ask how often he had introduced another woman to this environment. "It's as if you belong here. I keep wondering if it might be with me." He turned over onto his back and gazed up at the ceiling. "I know what we'll do today. How would you like to come to work with me?"

"I thought your work was in your airplane?"

"It is. Fishing season is over, hunting isn't starting up yet. This is the time we take the plane up, see if anything is shaking loose, get her ready to head back to work.

"Like our ranchers in San Amaro? They spend the winter mending equipment, fixing irrigation, getting ready for planting months in the future."

"Right. Except they're on the ground. We're going to be a few thousand feet above it."

Although she was often needlessly anxious behind the wheel of a car and refused to drive at all in the crowded, often steep maws of San Francisco, Annalee had never been fearful in an airplane. Now, as she faced being a passenger in fragile Blue Lady, she wondered if her comfort with being aloft was about to end.

"I'm going to show you how to get in," Rusty said. He led her to the right side of the aircraft and swung open a transparent door that appeared to have been made from Saran Wrap and wire. His tone was serious, almost businesslike. "You need to do this the same way each time. Put your right foot on the strut. This is the strut. Look at it first. Stand on it, it's OK. Now grab the pilot's seat with both hands and swing your left leg in. Now your right leg and sit down in the seat behind where I go. Don't touch that bar overhead; it's full of aviation fuel."

Annalee followed his instructions. The metal frame of Blue Lady was cool under her palms. The craft rocked slightly with her weight.

"I want you to get familiar with these straps," he continued. He held up belts and buckles that resembled those on commercial aircraft. But while one went across her lap (low and tight across my hips, Annalee said silently in a parody of a flight attendant), two more circled her shoulders. Rusty's hand grazed her thigh as he strapped her in. She glanced at him, ready for a seductive exchange and saw that his expression was solemn. "Now, this package holds survival gear," he continued. He reached behind her to hold up a thickly-wrapped package. "There's food, maps, a thermal blanket and a tent."

"In *there*?"

"You'd be amazed at how small they can make these things. And we're not going to be lost for very long. I'm pretty religious about filing a flight plan."

Annalee rolled her eyes. "Look, don't start acting like a cowboy and trying to scare me."

Rusty stopped and leaned against the aircraft's frame. "I'd never go off the ground without preparation any more than you'd drive a car with no fuel in the tank." His tone and expression were focused and intent. "In an airplane, that always means you prepare for something to go wrong. And when I'm at the controls I'm the boss and you listen to me."

"What if I don't want to," Annalee said, teasing him to lighten the tone.

"Then we're heading in the wrong direction." There was no mistaking his serious mien. Annalee realized this was no time for joking, flirting or banter. She felt her trust in Rusty open and deepen. His pilot persona cast him in a new light.

Rusty vaulted into the pilot's seat before her, obscuring her view of a bank of dials, controls, handles, switches and knobs.

"See the headset in the pouch right in front of you, behind my seat? Put it on over your ears and adjust the volume with the dials. You and I can talk, but if I hold my hand up it means I'm hearing something from the control tower or another pilot and we need to stop talking."

Beneath her feet and surrounding her, Annalee felt Blue Lady come to life. The sound of the engine was deafening and the frame began to vibrate. The propellers became a blur. Annalee clapped the headset to her ears and heard static, then the sound of Rusty's grainy southern voice giving coordinates to a flight tower invisible in the distance. She felt the ground move beneath the wheels and then a sensation of weightlessness unlike anything she had felt in a commercial airliner. She saw a spray of gravel and then, seemingly in increments of inches, the earth beneath them began to recede. She gripped the sides of her seat. The aircraft continued to vibrate and then gradually Annalee felt it smoothen around her. She risked opening her eyes. Before her she saw Rusty's denim shirt and shaggy hair, his profile as he turned his head to scan the horizon. He was smiling slightly as if he felt pleasure in flight. They were aloft. Annalee saw trees below growing smaller as they gained altitude.

Rusty's voice came over the headset. "Look down for just a moment, then look back."

Annalee did so. Below she saw a white field of snow, trees lifting up over hills, outcroppings stark and gray against the backdrop. "OK," she said. "What was I looking for."

"How do you feel?"

Annalee scanned her inner horizon. She still felt mildly anxious, but also invigorated. She felt curiosity and an increasing desire to remain in flight. Cautiously, she simply said, "I feel fine. Why?"

"I want to show you stuff on the ground as we go over it but some people can't stand to look down. It makes them dizzy and queasy. Are you sure you're OK?"

Annalee experimented. She looked down as Rusty piloted the airplane closer to the hills. "Yes, I'm sure." She saw, outlined in shadow, a white creature among the high rocks far below.

"Oh! Oh, look," she cried. "There's an animal down there. Is it a wolf?"

Rusty's laughter filled the headset. "I'm going to pretend it's altitude and not because you're a city girl who can't tell a wolf from a Dahl sheep."

For the next hour they circled hilltops, dipped down to view cirques, slowly crisscrossed glaciers. Annalee's comfort grew beyond acceptance. She wanted to stay forever high above the expanse of the Alaskan interior.

"You sure you don't mind all this rising and sinking? I've seen seasoned pilots who can't take it."

"I love it, Rusty. I just love it."

"That's what it takes to fit in here. You have to love it."

The short gravel strip behind the cabin made for a breathtakingly steep descent and bumpy landing but Annalee enjoyed even that experience. Later that night she awoke to appreciate the sight of Blue Lady resting on her landing strip, visible through the bedroom window in the moonlight.

Chapter 15

Ruth, Denise, Cheryl, Yvonne, Kim, Angela—and Especially Susan

On the seventh morning of Annalee's stay in Alaska, the missing pieces fell into place. Rusty's sexual skill, his slips alluding to many other women. The pink faux-feminine bathroom. On that morning Annalee learned about Susan. She also learned about Ruth, Denise, Cheryl, Yvonne, Kim and Angela but it was Susan who unwittingly taught Annalee how much she had changed.

Rusty would be gone for a few hours. He needed to find some parts for the airplane and install them, he explained. Annalee would be more comfortable staying at the cabin. After he left she experimentally thumbed through the classified ads in the small weekly newspaper from Fairbanks. She wasn't ready to reveal her thoughts to Rusty, but his questions about a future together had opened a dizzying possibility. Other than history, she had no compelling ties to San Amaro. Alaska was racing away with her heart and her feelings for Rusty were deepening. He was obviously interested in a serious relationship with her. In time she might live with him but she would always be financially independent. If she were to live in Alaska, what were her employment prospects? She saw classified ads for heavy machinery, well pump digging equipment, lumber, propane heaters and chain saws. There would be hardware stores. She would know most of the stock. Mud and cold and dust and rain were the same regardless of degree and Rusty could teach her about snow and ice.

Musing, she went to the pantry in search of a cup and the jar of coffee. The shelf was high and she needed to lift up on her toes. As she clumsily pulled down the jar she inadvertently took with it a hefty paper sack that rested on the corner. It fell to the floor and spilled its contents.

It appeared to hold a stack of letters in a variety of colors and weights.

Annalee looked at the splay of paper at her feet and then, holding her breath, reached down and lifted one envelope by its corner. The ink was pale mauve, handwriting was feminine, return address was somewhere in Indiana. She lifted the flap. The contents appeared to be photographs and a letter written in lavender on heavy cream stock. Annalee dropped the missive and came back to the table, still looking over her shoulder at the small avalanche on the floor.

So what? Of course Rusty had corresponded with women. It's how she met him, after all. And of course she wasn't the only *Alaskan Bachelors* reader to have responded to that seductive image, the wet fish, the innocently exposed navel. Clearly he was no longer involved with these correspondents. While he hadn't said so, not in so many words, he had all but asked her to move in with him. His hopes for a relationship with her revealed all she needed to know. To read mail that wasn't meant for her would violate every law of decency. A true friend, an honorable person, someone secure and healthy like herself would scoop those letters, slip them back into their bag and carefully return it to the shelf. She would do so. Now.

Annalee looked outside. At 10 a.m. the sun was merely a salmon pink band along the horizon. She gazed down into her empty cup and remembered that she was about to make coffee. She would brew a cup, drink it and return to the woods. By now she felt like an old hand at dressing for the elements. The borrowed layers of socks and sweaters were as familiar to her as if they were her own. Again the unwelcome thought. Just whose stacks of clothing did fill that closet? She walked back over to the letters and looked down. The topmost envelope bore a postmark from five weeks ago and the address was San Diego. Annalee opened the envelope and read the contents. Then, carefully, she folded it and went back for the rest.

Many of the letters were perfumed, some handwriting was childlike and the paper decorated with images of puppies and kittens. Some were literate, some humorous, some sarcastic, some pleading and pathetic. But almost all of the writers had had some significant contact with Rusty. Many had been here. Several expressed an interest in returning, as one said, "in my place and in your heart." And Rusty had met dozens of others in airports and coffee shops and restaurants and motel rooms up and down the western seaboard. One spoke of holding his hands over dinner in Seattle, another described the intriguing flecks of black in his green eyes, two more alluded to nights in his arms and the warmth of his skin. Envelopes with the oldest postmarks were the initial *Alaskan Bachelors* introductions. The most recent held small personal gifts and the notes referred to a conversation or rendezvous as recently as last month. None said farewell. When had these women been here? When had he gone to them? When had he materialized at their front doors or in their gardens or at the workplace as he had at H.A.G.L.?

Annalee reflected. Rusty had always been the one to call her. Because of work, he said. His location was unpredictable. I'll just bet it was, Annalee thought now. When he talked to her about Alaska and she felt so close she thought she could hear the sound of ice cracking on the Yukon River, was Rusty actually making a clandestine call from the Santa Cruz boardwalk south of San Francisco with a lover awaiting him on the beach? She read on, through the sun's zenith and the early November afternoon. Women in love, women in doubt, widows of Viet Nam veterans, divorcees, inmates, the frank desperation, the feigned disinterest, the tender honesty. A political science instructor, a photographer who claimed to work for *National Geographic,* a kindergarten teacher, one female shepherd from Oregon. Annalee realized that she was clenching her teeth and consciously slackened her jaw.

It was 1 p.m. and shadows had lengthened from the birch tree beside the cabin when the phone rang. A sense of déjà vu, of the moment when she answered the phone to Aura—it seemed a lifetime ago—caused her to smile grimly. And sure enough.

"Hi, sweetheart," a woman's voice said through the answering machine's speaker. "Listen, Rita called, that agent from Greatlands Realty. She thinks she found a place for us. I know your aunt is visiting from California but maybe Kenny and Katie can baby sit her tomorrow so we can see it. I'd like to meet Rita in person since we'll be working with her. My stuff will get here in two more weeks and it would be great if we had our own place before it shows up. Oh, and Jason thinks he left his

Walkman back at the hospital in Fairbanks, so can we pick it up? The little shit is driving me crazy. Next time he falls off a roof, you and I ain't taking him to the E.R. He can splint his ankle himself. Oh hell, what are teenagers for besides to scare the crap out of their mothers. Anyway, love you, baby. See you tomorrow."

When Rusty returned a half hour later, stamping his feet in the mud room, Annalee met him with her duffle bag packed, arms folded and eyes narrowed to slits. She deliberately parroted her own words from six years ago. "Your girlfriend called. She had a lot to say . . . ."

They sat across from one another at the kitchen table. The walrus skull on the wall, backlit from a fire in the living room hearth, cast its long tusked shadow over Rusty's features. His hands were folded between his knees, eyes downcast. He was going to be honest with her, he said. He had deserved every moment of her shouting outrage, he was surprised she had only yelled at him and had not killed him, but he could explain everything if she would just give him a chance.

Annalee realized she was, in a small way, a hostage. She had no idea how to get back to the airport herself, or how to describe Rusty's location to a taxi driver if indeed there was a taxi anywhere within a 20 mile radius. So she would simply sit through the monologue.

"This is how it is, Annalee. The whole story. Now, I had my share of sex back in the sixties. It was the Summer of Love and you know how things were back then . . . ."

Annalee groaned inwardly. Apparently his soliloquy would span two decades.

"Those Georgia country girls weren't savvy like the ladies where you're from in San Francisco but they still felt those good vibrations. I had a great time and I think they did too. And sure I got hurt but not bad, even after Lauralee divorced me . . . ."

Annalee wondered if the socks she was wearing were her own or from the closet.

" . . . And then, Annalee, I met the love of my life." He gestured toward the window. "That's her. Out there. Alaska. I always wanted to fly and there wasn't much opportunity in Georgia back then. I knew up here flying is almost as ordinary as driving a car so I moved on up and after a few years...."

She would donate her arctic gear to the homeless shelter in San Amaro, Annalee decided. A homeless person would appreciate the duffle bag.

"... when it comes to money and flying and the outdoors, Alaska is everything a man could want. But as far as women went, well, what can I say. It sucked. Once in awhile, I admit, I'd spend a few nights with this lady whose husband worked the pipeline or another's fished along the coast all season." But, he said, most of the time the Last Frontier was a howling tundra when it came to sex. And for him celibacy was tougher than any hardship wrought by work or weather.

Annalee wondered if she could just show up at the airport and exchange her return ticket which was for Sunday. This was only Thursday.

"... then Kenny brings me this-here bachelor magazine."

Annalee wiggled one foot as Rusty rambled. She knew the next twist in the tale. She had been part of it. His profile had appeared in the very issue when *Alaskan Bachelors*, the newest phenomenon in the burgeoning Baby Boomer singles scene, went national on the afternoon and late-night talk shows and captured the attention of thousands of women, Ivy among them. The publication quickly sank back into obscurity but in those heady months of its success the high glacial wall that stood between Rusty and sexual intercourse splintered and cracked. And then, in a roaring avalanche, the mail flooded into tiny Garnet. "The post office lady had to keep one bag under my mailbox and one under Kenny's for all the letters."

Annalee counted the antlers in the room. There were 18 and a moose's furry ears were noticeably dusty. How did one dust a moose?

"... So Annalee, what was I supposed to do? They were all nice ladies. There were a lot of them and it seemed rude not to write back or at least send a card."

A card. Evelyn's birthday was next week. Annalee would send her a card. She yawned.

Rusty took a deep breath and forged ahead. "So I'd call them and next thing I know they're in love with me. I really started to like a few of them and we'd write or talk. My phone bills were up in the triple digits but some of those ladies were so pretty and they kept themselves up so good. Like you." Rusty's glance met Annalee's flat stare. "And so I just kept going. I was like a kid in a candy store...."

Oh, a candy store! There was a curious little candy store in San Amaro, Annalee recalled fondly. Many Happy Returns was a cult favorite among local Baby Boomers for its impressive stock of retro candy from the 1950s and 1960s. Annalee's mouth watered. She would go there for a Sky Bar next week.

"...didn't just write to me from America. There were Japanese ladies and some from India too. It was fun at first. I'd spend every night writing or talking to them and all day Sunday...."

Next Sunday, her day off, perfect for a visit to Many Happy Returns. People-watching there was as great a pleasure as selecting and eating a treat. On Sunday the throngs of middle-aged customers would spill out onto the sidewalk. Did the 45 year old investment broker of today pine for a strip of the candy buttons that would turn his fingers pink and green when he was ten? He could find those paper ribbons at Many Happy Returns and willingly handed over $5 for the item that had cost him five cents as a child.

"...started to get crazy. I got letters from teenagers who wanted to meet me and a seventy year old grandmother...."

Annalee remembered the buffed grandmother who led the Sleek And Silver aerobics class at the San Amaro gym, looking guilty as she paid for her rock candy on a string at Many Happy Returns. And there was Bit-O-Honey, Nick-L-Lips with fruit juice in wax bottles, Allsorts with their layers of licorice and unidentifiable white and pink substance.

"...Some of the ladies wanted a boyfriend. Some were looking for a secret affair or a husband or a baby or just a sugar daddy...."

Sugar Daddies, that succulent caramel on a stick. And Sugar Babies, Milk Duds, Neck-O-Wafers and, most clandestine of all, chocolate cigarettes and bubble gum cigars.

"When I was younger I just took sex for granted, then there was nothing for so long, then I got to make up for the last twenty years. It was like the sixties except by now those ladies knew their way around the bedroom. But it got out of hand." Now Rusty was describing the penalty. His indulgence came with a hefty price. Like candy he savored, he swallowed, he adored almost every morsel. But he was left with dire emotional obligations. The relationships which began so sweetly began to tear and rend his peace of mind the way hard Christmas candy could lacerate a tongue.

Annalee's glance met the hollow eye sockets of the walrus. She imagined they shared a shrug. She was finished.

"We all know right from wrong, Rusty. Face it. You took advantage of vulnerable women." Her attention turned to the now-familiar view outside of branches bending in the breeze that came up from the river. She scanned the sky. Wispy clouds, not dark, no precipitation today, wind coming from the east. She had learned so much about Alaska and now she would be leaving. She felt a pang of sadness.

"Maybe I was vulnerable too," Rusty said into the silence.

"Oh, I'm sure you were. But it doesn't excuse or explain the way you used women. Or let's just focus on one woman at a time. Me."

"I never used you."

"No? 'I don't know how I can pack you up, Annalee,'" she quoted. "'Just keep an open mind about me, Annalee.' 'Can you see yourself living here some day, Annalee? I keep thinking it might be with me.' And all the while Susan with her son is down the road lining up realtors and probably a minister for the wedding." In spite of herself Annalee's eyes welled up. "You told her I was your maiden aunt! And then you came back here and had sex with me. What was it if not using me? And her."

"It was sudden and I couldn't stop her. She was like a runaway train."

"Sudden? As in, packing up her belongings, traveling to Alaska with her son, finding a place to live, getting cozy enough to scout for property to buy with you? That must have taken her a speed-of-light six months. Why didn't you tell me, Rusty?"

"She and I had a thing down in Santa Cruz. It was when I came back through San Amaro. Even by then things with her and me weren't going well. She was so sweet at first, but man did she change. She gets really emotional, reminds me of my sister Sheena Kay. That girl, once she gets upset she goes off the rails. You never see it coming. And, well, I was never that good with talking to women." Annalee snorted. "So I figured

I'd back off and she'd get the message. I slowed down on writing to her, didn't call back, and right around that time was when you phoned me up out of the blue and said Alaska was making you crazy. You weren't hung up on me, it seemed to be all about Alaska. If there's any feeling I understand, it's that one about Alaska. I wanted you to be here. After awhile it was you that was making me crazy. And then all of a sudden, here's Susan. I didn't want to lose you but I couldn't figure out how to tell her without her getting all wound up the way she does. She threw a flower pot at me in Santa Cruz when I wanted to leave a day early, and she goes bat-crap crazy any time her kid does something wrong. Yes, I did know she was looking for a place to live here but I never said it was with me.

"OK, so I'm a coward and I fucked up. And yes, other women were here and I met a lot of the others down there. But once we got to know each other it turned out that they didn't like Alaska, or me, or they had too much baggage or wanted me to rescue them or I just didn't take to them. Except for a few of them we never really got involved enough to break up. We just sort of faded out of each other's lives. Hell, it was fun to talk to the ladies and meet them. I can't help it if they went on fantasy trips about me. I just figured we were chit-chatting and all of a sudden they're pissed off and acting like I made promises."

Rusty puffed out his cheeks as if he were about to inflate a balloon and then released his breath. "Man, I had no idea women could be so undercover. I mean, at least with my ex and my sisters, especially Sheena Kay, once they work up a head of steam you see them coming like a freight train. But these other ladies, Susan most of all, they sneak up and bite you in the butt. And *then* here comes the freight train."

Annalee had seen women in San Amaro do just this, set their sights on a man and then manipulate and scheme to "land" him, as they shamelessly disclosed. And her relationship with Rusty was colored and complicated by her feelings for Alaska, the way it held her in thrall but never seemed within reach itself.

"Then here's my part in this," she said. Rusty folded his arms and leaned back in his chair. "Starting last March when we would talk on the phone, I was interested in you. But with Alaska it was more than just interest. It was like something took hold of me but I didn't know what it was." Piecing her way through the emotions that had consumed her, Annalee found the words. "When I'm here in the cabin I think, no, this is simply water and earth, ice and snow, trees and the tracks of animals. That's all. This landscape would look the same in Canada, Russia, Norway. But when I'm standing out there on the river bank I feel as if it senses and judges me. I wonder, is this what you men experience when you're with one of those beautiful, unattainable women, the kind who always invite a chase, always outdistance and lure you on? I want to chase it and . . . not tame it but win its approval." Annalee glanced at Rusty and saw him fighting a smile. She felt a flush of embarrassment and disappointment. "Forget it. Let's get going. I have a plane to catch."

"I'm not laughing at you, Annalee. I'm remembering the first time I felt that way. Alaska caught you. It caught me. It happens with certain people. It has nothing to do with the beauty or fishing or the other tourist crap. With certain of us, once Alaska catches us we have to stay or keep coming back. It's like alcohol to a drunk. You can swear off but it's always going to be waiting out there on the horizon for you to fall off the wagon. Here." Rusty went to a shelf piled with airplane manuals, gun catalogues, leather working tools and part of an antler. He returned with a book, slim, worn and musty, opened it to a dog-eared page and slid the volume to her.

"What's this," she asked. "Homework?"

"Just look at it."

She glanced at the spine. "The Spell Of The Yukon," she said. "By Robert Service. Never heard of him." She flipped to the foreword and laughed with derision. "Poetry by a Yukon gold miner in 1906? Just missed getting the Pulitzer, no doubt."

"Please? Just read the one I showed you."

Exasperated, she read at first just to pass another few moments and then with a sense of comprehension and finally with a chill across her shoulders. Now and then she glanced over at Rusty. He was motionless, gazing at her intently with his elbows on the table and his chin on his hands. Twice she read the poem. She felt that it captured, laid open and exposed her thoughts and emotions. She voiced the last lines to hear the words aloud. "There's a land, oh, it beckons and beckons. And I want to go back. And I will."

She closed the book. Through the window she saw a flock of Canada geese lift from somewhere downstream and fly overhead in a streamlined V. Like ice, a fissure opened into her future and she risked a glance down into its unknown. She did want to come back. She suspected that her want would become need and that she would return. Without another soul to teach her how to manage the demands of Alaska, it would be better to have Rusty as an ally than an enemy. For that to happen she would need to trust him even if merely as a resource. If there was to be anything more, reconnecting would not leave him a hole to slither through.

"If you want to be with me, I want you to come clean with Susan and I want to hear it for myself. I don't trust you. Take me to see her."

Rusty looked stricken. "Oh Annalee, please don't ask for that. You have no idea what that woman is like. I never promised anything to Susan. Hell, I never promised anything to you but I will now. I'll promise to do whatever you want so that you can be here. With or without me. When Alaska caught me I didn't know anyone here and I learned things the hard way. I nearly died once or twice before I got the hang of black ice, mother bears and what it means to see fog on the horizon. We'll take it one day at a time. Either of us can back out, but we can try."

"It shouldn't have to be this hard, so that we have to try."

"Annalee, relationships take work. Haven't you ever had to try?"

Annalee felt her breath catch in her throat. Rusty might not be eloquent but he was accurate. She had never tried. She watched a shadow moving on the opposite shore and tracked the slow movement of an animal as it searched for nourishment in the brush. All around her the moment turned as above ground the day creatures shifted toward slumber and those in crevasses and caves sighed, deep in hibernation.

Rusty continued. "You haven't told me everything about you either. When I'm with you I feel like I'm more *with* you than any other woman, but I don't think you're with me. Not even when you're sitting here, like now." Annalee turned to Rusty and raised her eyebrows. "Sometimes I think you're in love with Alaska and I'm just the crash pad you came to stay at. Maybe you're the one using me. But when I feel like you're brushing me off it makes me want to chase you even more. It's like my ma said, I want what I can't have. I guess that's part of why I stay here.

Like you said, Alaska is like a woman but she's one I can never have. You remind me of Alaska that way. I don't think I can ever have you. But I'll settle for what I can get."

Annalee felt the balance of power in the relationship shift and shift again as if she and Rusty were on a ship tossed by waves, fighting for a foothold. "If I said you could have me, Rusty, you'd run away. You wouldn't be interested in a woman you couldn't chase."

"You might say that to me, that I could have you. But you'd be lying."

"All right, Rusty. You want to work on a relationship with me? I'll stay here until Sunday like I planned and then I'll go home. But I'll consider coming back as long as you know there are no promises. And I want to meet Susan."

"Can I call her on the phone? You can listen on the other line. Annalee, you don't know that woman. Like I keep saying, she gets really emotional."

"No, not over the phone." Annalee felt sorry for Susan. She remembered her own emotions when she was the abandoned one. For a week after Brad left her eyes felt like desert sand until she could finally cry. And once she started she felt as if she were drowning. It would be even more rocky for Susan, to go through this experience so far from home, knowing no one and with a teenager in tow.

"How do I know you won't dump me after I've gone through this?" Rusty asked.

"You don't."

Chapter 16

The Pyromaniac

It was 10 a.m. and snowing the next day when Annalee and Rusty entered a decrepit trailer park on the outskirts of a nearby settlement. It seemed deserted except for a scruffy cat that eyed them from under a rusting red Camaro. The car was parked before a single-wide mobile home. "Guess Susan's here," Rusty murmured. He backed his truck in beside the vehicle and they approached. Annalee noted the odor of mildew and cat urine and the sound of heavy metal music. Rusty rang the bell, there was indistinct shouting, the music stopped and the door was opened by a slender woman in bunny slippers, wool socks, ankle warmers, leopard-print stretch pants, a chenille scarf and what appeared to be several sweaters under a ski parka with a hood. Her nose was red and her upper lip was raw and damp. She held a box of Kleenex in one hand. With her jet black hair, raptor-like scarlet fingernails and matching lipstick, to Annalee she looked like every tough girl in high school who had competed with her for the love of Brad. The woman dabbed at her nose with a tissue and glanced from Rusty to Annalee. Her expression hovered between bewilderment and pleasure and settled on an uncertain smile.

"Wow, whad a dice surprise," she said to Rusty. And to Annalee, "I'b so glad to fidally beet you id persod."

"You're glad to meet me?" Annalee was nonplused.

Susan noisily blew her nose. "Come on in. You guys want a beer?"

"No, Susan," Rusty said. "Let's sit down and talk."

Susan ushered them in to an overly heated living room. It was dominated by a massive Wolfe tanning bed that shared an electrical outlet with a dusty television balanced on a stack of cinder blocks. "I can't get the hang of this goddamned furnace. I set it to 85 degrees and I'm still freezing." The other furniture consisted of a mustard yellow couch on a rag rug, a recliner and a metal TV tray. Annalee noted faux wood paneling peeling from the walls.

"God, I did not expect you. But this is great. Sit yourselves down." Susan grinned at Annalee, showing yellowed teeth. "It must be hard to drive around all day with the roads so slippery and stuff."

Annalee searched in vain for meaning. Finally she said, "I haven't been driving. Uh, Susan . . . ."

"Shut the fuck up, you little shit," Susan cried, "or I'll slam your head against the wall."

Annalee gasped. Then she noticed that Susan's eyes had shifted toward the hallway. The sound of Metallica and someone chanting along with the angry lyrics abruptly ceased.

"My son is having a hard time staying in his room. But we gotta get his ankle healed up. He just won't turn off that ghetto music. The little bastard. So, gosh, this is exciting. What do you have for me?"

Annalee attempted to get her heart rate back to normal. "What do I have for you?"

"Yeah. You said you might of found a house for me and Rusty?"

Comprehension dawned. The woman believed Annalee was the real estate agent who had been shopping for the house she would share with Rusty.

Now Susan was gazing at Annalee through narrowed eyes. "You are just the cutest thing. Rita, right?" Annalee's heart rate speeded up again. She eyed Susan's fingernails. "Hey, you better watch out or Rusty might hit on you. He's quite a player. Ain't you, Rust?"

"Sue, we need to talk," he said.

But Susan's eyes remained fixed on Annalee. With one hand she shook a cigarette from a pack on the end table and lit it with a practiced flick of the wrist. "Funny," she said slowly. "Your voice. On the phone you talked like you were from New York but now you don't have that accent." The music and chanting began again from somewhere out of sight. "Don't you two go nowhere." Susan was still smiling but with narrowed eyes and closed lips. Then she strode from the room. Seconds later the music stopped and the sound of an object hitting a wall rang through the air. Another crash reached Annalee's ears, then a stream of invective. Annalee's eyes were dry and she realized she had been afraid to blink. Quietly she stood and tiptoed toward the door.

"Do what you want," she whispered to Rusty over her shoulder. "I'm getting out of here."

He fell into step beside her. The hair rose on the back of her neck as she swiftly crossed the floor and flung open the trailer door. Then, slipping and sliding on the icy concrete walkway she and Rusty raced to his truck, leaped in, and they rolled out of the trailer park and onto the main road.

Annalee heard a soft snuffling. For an instant she thought Rusty was weeping. Then his laughter filled the cab. "You should have seen your face. You looked like she was pointing an AK-47 at you."

"If she had an AK-47 we'd both look like Swiss cheese right now. That wasn't funny, Rusty. The woman is psycho. You should have warned me."

"But I did!" Rusty glanced over at her. "I told you twenty times. Susan gets emotional."

With a sigh Annalee realized that to Rusty, "emotional" described any expression of feeling from homicidal mania to comatose depression.

"Remember how I told you I was seeing her in Santa Cruz and when I went to leave early she threw a jar of flowers at me? If that's not emotional, what is? And I don't think her kid's black eye came from a schoolyard fight like she said."

As Annalee feared the light was blinking on Rusty's answering machine when they entered his cabin. The phone rang and Rusty grimaced at it and picked up.

"Look, Su.... Who? Do I know you? Oh, right. Rita, from Greatlands Realty. No, I guess we never met. Uh huh. Upset, yes. That was my friend Annalee. Well, Susan's not my fiancée. No, not buying property together. I can't help what she told you. See, Rita, the thing about Susan is that she, she, uh, she..."

"Gets emotional," Annalee supplied from her side of the table.

Rusty nodded. "She gets emotional. It turned into a big goddamned mess. Right. I'm sorry for the hassle, Rita. Yes, thanks. Goodbye." He hung up, folded his arms on the table and put his head down. "Go ahead, say it." His voice was muffled. "The famous saying about single men in Alaska. The odds are good, but the goods are odd."

"That's what they should have named the magazine."

"Now, can we put this thing with Susan and the other ladies behind us?"

"No promises, Rusty. No promises."

⁓

They left early the next morning to fly several hours north. A friend was delayed in Oregon and he asked Rusty to check on his homestead deep in the interior. They found the cabin encircled by bear tracks but evidently the creature hadn't broken in and was probably hibernating. Now Rusty dipped low over the treetops and turned Blue Lady for home. To Annalee the landscape far below looked featureless with hour after hour of white-blanketed hills and evergreen forests.

"How do you know where you are?" she asked.

"I've flown this route a million times. After awhile the landscape looks as familiar as my living room." The plane bucked, sunk and rose again in a pocket of turbulence. "Are you white-knuckling the edges of your seat?" Rusty's voice through the headset was tinny but she could hear the smile in his tone.

"I'm not. I feel as if I never want to come down to earth."

"Maybe you trust me now?"

"You're no danger to me up here unless you decide to crash. And then we'd both be in trouble."

"Guess you never heard of the mile-high club." Rusty dipped the small plane over a low pinnacle and Annalee saw several Dahl sheep look up to watch their passing. "The club for people who have sex while they're flying. Wanna try?"

"What are you, in junior high? I can't believe anyone smart enough to fly an airplane would be that immature."

Rusty was silent. For a moment Annalee wondered if he was serious and how anyone could, or would want to, have sex at 4,000 feet while both were strapped down with safety belts that crossed their laps, shoulders and chests. Rusty was a cautious pilot and seemed to respect flight and airplanes.

"Rusty? You were joking, right?"

Rusty responded but his tone was serious. "I'm going to open the window for a second. I need to check something out. Brace yourself for a breeze."

"You're opening the window? While we're flying? Now I am scared."

"I do it all the time when I'm working. The window distorts my vision so I fly with it open for hours. Hang on."

To Annalee the sudden blast whipping past her ears seemed like a hurricane. "What are you looking for?" she called.

He held up his hand momentarily to silence her, then shouted over the wind. "Right now I'm not looking. I'm smelling. Give me a moment. I need to focus."

They flew. The wind stung Annalee's eyes. Her hair would be a mare's nest when they landed. Now she was in fact gripping the edges of her seat, afraid to let go and tuck her curls back into her hood. She wished they would land. Nothing seemed amiss but Rusty knew every nut and bolt in Blue Lady. After several moments of anxiety she risked interrupting again. "Is something wrong with the engine?"

"Does the air look smoky to you? Do you smell anything?"

Annalee squinted and inhaled. To her unpracticed eye the environment seemed no different than it had an hour ago. The wind filled her nostrils and she found it difficult to inhale. Thankfully Rusty closed the window.

"I don't see or smell anything. What's wrong?"

Rusty was silent but she felt the engine surge and Blue Lady picked up speed. In seconds she realized that the air had in fact turned a delicate shade of taupe. In California throughout late spring and into the fall this haze could fill the air for miles when forest fires in the deep, steep remote canyons would scrc the landscape and create havoc for firefighters. Strange season for a burn, she mused. Surely the snow would extinguish a blaze. "Is there a fire, Rusty?"

"Holy shit. Look down there." Rusty pointed ahead. The landscape now was familiar. There was the road they took to the store, the neighbor with the green John Deere truck. The distant end of Rusty's landing strip appeared. Annalee saw the cabin. She looked and looked again in disbelief. Smoke seeped from Rusty's bedroom window. Aghast, she saw a tongue of flame lick out and blacken the frame.

Now Rusty had forced the engine to full throttle and was speeding down at what seemed to be a nearly vertical angle. Annalee closed her eyes and prayed until she felt the landing gear touch the ground. The impact jarred her teeth and the craft rattled to a halt, spraying gravel. Rusty had unhooked his safety belts before the propeller had stopped, opened the airplane door, vaulted out and ran.

"Can you get out OK?" he called over his shoulder.

"Keep going! I'll catch up with you!"

Rusty had reached the rear of the cabin and was uncoiling a thick black hose from an insulated shed as Annalee raced up to join him. "If the water's frozen we're screwed!" he cried. Annalee saw the hose stiffen as water filled and flowed from the nozzle. There was no time to feel relief.

"What should I do?" she shouted over the hiss of water.

"Go get Andy! Head down to the river and bang hard on the metal bucket. He'll come to the back door. Point to the cabin and he'll see the smoke. Wait, here he comes now!"

An extended cab pickup with a gun rack roared into view and slid to a halt. A burly man with a stark white handlebar mustache, long white beard, stunning white dreadlocks under a cowboy hat and a deeply lined face leaped from the vehicle and thudded toward them. He carried a fire extinguisher in one hand and an ax in the other. He looked like an unlikely meld of Santa Claus, Willie Nelson and a Caucasian version of Bob Marley.

"Damned good thing I was chopping wood out back or I'd-a never seen the smoke," he gasped. "Let's let 'er have it."

Annalee stepped aside and waited. The men worked silently, in tandem, dousing the smoke and flames. It seemed as if hours had passed when they finally stopped, exchanged a glance, nodded and surveyed the blackened cabin.

"Looks like only half got damaged," the man named Andy observed.

"Just the bedroom end, maybe the bathroom," Rusty said. "I don't understand it. The wiring's good. And I'd never leave the place with a fire going. That fireplace is lined in stone anyway. There's just nothing in there that would have caught."

"Uh, Rusty, I seen some lady go down your road like a bat about an hour ago."

"Lady?"

"Drove a beater red Camaro that looked all shot to hell."

Rusty folded his arms across his chest and looked into the distance. "I don't believe it. I do not fucking believe it." His voice was husky, nearly a whisper.

"What was it, somebody got pissed off at you? Wasn't this-here lady, was it?"

He smiled at Annalee who found her face too frozen with horror to respond.

"No. It wasn't." Rusty finally tore his gaze from the ruined half of his cabin. "Annalee, this is Andy. Andy, Annalee."

Andy took both of Annalee's hands in his and gave them a brief squeeze. His touch was surprisingly soft.

"Well," Rusty said, "I suppose we'd better go in."

He led the way with Andy behind him and Annalee bringing up the rear. He opened the door and then, in a parody of Annalee's first moment at the cabin, he inhaled, stepped back and collided with Andy. Annalee peered around them. The walrus skull, the pride of Rusty's head collection, lay shattered on the floor. Across its tusks was smeared a red substance. It was the shade of scarlet that had caused Annalee panic when she glimpsed Susan's lethal-looking fingernails. Annalee imagined the woman lurking in the underbrush with a bottle of nail polish, kerosene and matches at the ready, waiting for her chance. The three stood in the doorway, agape and motionless.

Finally Andy interrupted the silence. "I can get that sucker back in shape. Walrus skull, hell, it ain't nothin' but bone." He socked Rusty on the shoulder in a male equivalent of a tender hug. "Give me a week, that fool thing will be good as new. Just a skull like this with no skin is a cinch." The neighbor turned to Annalee. "I don't like to brag on myself but other folks said it first. I'm not bad at my job, and that's taxidermy." Annalee resisted an urge to wipe her palms on her jacket and wondered if Andy had been skinning a moose before they shook hands. They stood for another moment. Then Rusty said, "I've got something to take care of. Andy, would you take Annalee home with you?"

Andy said "sure" at the same moment Annalee cried, "what?"

Rusty placed his hands on her shoulders and looked hard into her eyes. "Annalee, I'm going to be gone for awhile. You can't stay here alone. Not without heat, and with a hole burned in the roof." Annalee was mindful of the darkness settling and the cold wind around her shoulders. "Andy here will take you on over to his place."

"You bet I will! It's your lucky day, Annalee," the man boomed. "I'm brewing up a mean kettle of stew. Meat's so tender you can cut it with a fork. You can't believe moose could be like butter but mine is! Put some 'taters in it too. You're in for a real treat, young lady."

Annalee's knees felt weak. She was still in shock from the fire and now she dreaded what she would face at the home of a taxidermist. She had always been more squeamish than most. In high school she had failed biology class. At the first sight of a long-dead frog on the dissecting table she had fainted and from then on couldn't enter the room without swooning. And she averted her eyes from the display case at Vera's Market when the sign advertised rabbit for stew. Would she stumble over some vestige of a dismembered animal at the home of a taxidermist, lose consciousness and cause him to administer the Heimlich Maneuver—or whatever someone did with a guest who had passed out? As they walked toward Andy's truck, like a slide show her imagination flipped through a running stream of frights she might find. Blood, fur, innards . . . dear God, ears. Andy hoisted himself into the driver's seat and Rusty leaned on the passenger side door as Annalee settled in. "I'll be back," he said quietly. His eyes looked haunted.

⁓

Annalee hoped the drive to Andy's would somehow offer an opportunity to mention that her sensitivity to gore was not up to Alaskan standards."

"So where you from, young lady?"

"Northern California, the wine country, we don't have taxidermists there," she said desperately. "I could never be a taxidermist. You see . . . ."

"Oh hell, it's easy once you know what to do." Andy looked over at her with a broad grin and his eyes alight. "I started with rabbits when I was eight. My daddy taught me and his daddy taught him. Things is different now though. Like, you get your big game hunter wanna-be from down to the Lower 48? Some Yuppie guy in a three-piece suit? And he comes up to Alaska to go hunting like a real man and next thing you know he's shot the holy shit out of some poor Dahl sheep because he don't know better than to use a shotgun. Man!" Andy guffawed and pounded the steering wheel with both ham-like hands. "They bring me some poor critter ain't much left of, looks like a sieve, got about 16 tons of shotgun lead in his side, bled out all over someone's goddamned rental truck."

"Imagine that," Annalee said. Her stomach heaved and she felt faint.

"Yeah. And likely the guy's all bit up with skeeters, half drunk, wants me to make the poor fucking, whoa, oops, make the poor sheep look like a leopard that was gonna bite him on the neck and drag him up a tree for dinner." Annalee was afflicted with a surreal mental image of a sheep dragging an unfortunate hunter up a tree. "But hell. It might take extra time but I don't charge the poor guy nothin' to pick the shot out. I like to sew it up nice, get the eyes in right. Even tilt the neck down like it's gonna charge. The poor sucker can go back to New Yawk with a big story about how he nearly got killed by this dangerous sheep." Here Andy paused and shook his head mournfully. "You can't eat the meat, though. Them guys don't know how to dress their kill. It's a cryin' shame. Alls you have to do is slice it nice and easy from its neck down to its asshole and take out everything from there on down. If you leave the glands in, next thing you know the meat tastes like ... What's the matter, you lose something?"

"I think I dropped an earring," Annalee murmured. She was doubled over with her hair touching the truck's floorboards. The nurse at the high school infirmary would always advise her to drop her head down between her knees this way to keep herself from passing out. "I drop earrings all the time. It must be here somewhere." Then she heard the crunch of tires on gravel, peeked up to see a neat cabin surrounded by pines, and braced for the worst.

"You like blueberries in your salad? I do."

In the shelter of Andy's living room Annalee was huddled under a comforter. "Love them," she called. So far she had not seen tendons, eyeballs or mammalian fluids. If anything Andy's home seemed almost antiseptic. There was the ubiquitous elk head on the wall, with antlers. There was the ram's head. And a moose, also antlered. And a selection of trophies showing that Andy coached the Fairbanks Junior Softball League which had apparently mopped the floor with the Juneau league in 1988. Other than those insignia, Andy could have been any of her customers at H.A.G.L. Nothing suggested this was the home of a man who spent his life shuffling around in carcasses.

Annalee cast off her comforter and padded to the kitchen. She found Andy in an apron with a sailor hat at an angle on his long white hair. He was tossing greens, tomatoes, Parmesan and blueberries in a wooden salad bowl. Something fragrant bubbled in a cauldron-sized cast iron pot on the stove.

"Wish I had some wine for a lady from the wine country," Andy said. "But we'll have to make do with lager."

"Hey, I could use a break from all that darn wine," Annalee said with a smile. "Beer is just fine for me. And dinner smells heavenly." She surreptitiously glanced around his kitchen. She saw no drops of blood on the floor or fur in the sink. "Andy, I'm curious. Where do you do your, um, taxidermy?" Perhaps it was in another own. Or, if that was too good to be hoped, maybe in an outbuilding. Within sight but not very close.

"Downstairs," Andy said. He jerked his thumb toward a door in the kitchen. "Had the garage enlarged so I can get any size truck in there. Guys with bear, moose, what have you, they can just back up and drive on in. Then the overhead winch slides the kill down to a pit in the concrete. Once we finish dressing 'er out, I get the guys to move the hell out of my way so I can do the real work." One again, Andy's eyes were alight. Annalee grasped the edge of the dining room table.

Dinner was aromatic and plentiful. Andy, looking proud, spooned ladles of stew into Annalee's bowl. Salad was crisp and green and the mug of frothy amber beer complemented the range of colors and flavors. Annalee gazed down into her bowl and noted cubes of potatoes, tiny bubbles of fat, carrots, celery and chunks of meat she assumed were moose. The aroma was indescribable. Yet, even as she salivated and acknowledged the rumbling of her stomach, empty since breakfast long ago, her florid imagination presented a mental slide show of the basement below. There, under a dim unshaded bulb like a scene from an old horror movie, the taxidermy shop. She imagined a coroner's metal table and the carcass of a creature with matted fur and red-rimmed sightless eyes. A yeti! Not quite dead, it would rise from the table and slowly.... Obviously not a yeti, she chastised herself. Just a moose. Like the one whose mortal remains were in the bowl before her. A moose with hooves, those hairy ears, a snout....

"Dinner OK?" Andy's question broke into her lurid fantasies. "You don't seem hungry."

"I guess I'm just upset about the fire," Annalee said weakly. She pushed her bowl away.

"Hey, tell you what. Let's take you down to see my shop! That'll work you up an appetite. You ain't never seen anything like my granddaddy's wood and bone needles that he used when he sewed up the hides by hand a hundred years ago." Andy pushed his chair aside and lumbered toward the basement door, motioning Annalee to follow. "You'll really have a story to tell when you get back to California."

Annalee wondered if there was a way she might spontaneously break a femur en route to the basement. She reached the stairwell with her bones intact and had no choice. Narrowing her eyes to slits as she did when she watched a scary movie, she slowly made her way hand over hand along the banister toward the basement and reached the floor. She was bracing to raise her eyes to whatever horror would confront her when a blur of motion crossed her peripheral vision. She was aware of speed, a mound of shaggy fur and panting. A massive black form crashed into her side, Andy cried, "Bear! No!" and Annalee fainted. Just before she lost consciousness she felt something salty, sticky and wet cross her lips.

Chapter 17

No Promises

 Annalee regained her senses before she regained her logic. She smelled a fishy odor, the air seemed fetid, her cheeks were wet and she felt a cool slick surface under her head. She wondered if she were on a ship, and came fully conscious on Andy's leather couch with the big man hovering over her, wide-eyed and wringing his hands. At his side, eyes equally wide, tongue lolling, panting fishy breath, with a silver string of drool hanging from his lower jaw was the largest dog Annalee had ever seen. Andy was addressing her and the animal equally in a breathless monotone.

 "Jesus, lady, you're scaring the crap out of me. Shove over, Bear. I knew I should have tied you up outside. Did you hit your head when he pushed you down? How many times have I told you not to jump on people? Crap, Rusty trusts me with his lady friend for two minutes and my dog kills her. For the love of God, quit slobbering. Please talk to me. Go downstairs and eat, you big clumsy goofball . . . ."

 "I'm OK." Annalee sat up gingerly and reached out to pat the animal's wooly head. "What a beautiful dog. Is he friendly?" Andy's answer was irrelevant. At her touch the creature launched himself toward her and covered her face with slimy kisses. Annalee was still shaky but able to laugh.

 Andy pointed toward the cellar door. "Go, Bear. You can visit Annalee later." The huge animal padded to the cellar door and went down the stairs. "He's the greatest old guy. He loves the ladies but he doesn't get to see any since Margaret died of cancer four years ago and the girls went off to college in Seattle. I take him everywhere. You can't believe a big critter like that can be so quiet in the woods. I swear his paws don't touch the ground when he's tracking, and he won't touch the kill even though you can tell he wants to. He just sits there watching with his eyes all shiny."

Annalee, seeing another visual image of a carcass, moaned. Andy looked alarmed.

"Why don't you just lie back down and have a little nap? It's been a bad day. I'm gonna finish up in the kitchen, have a bit more stew."

Just before she resurfaced from sleep Annalee dreamed that she was at her counter at H.A.G.L. facing Santa Claus who was reeling off a shopping list of building supplies. But instead of lumber and nails she was handing him a rack of antlers, an armload of shaggy fur and a bowl of stew in which a tiny moose was singing "Nearer My God To Thee." She opened her eyes.

"About thirty sheets of drywall," she heard, "at least ten pounds of four inch nails, two-by-fours, fifty feet of insulation . . . ."

"You're going to paint and tape, right?"

"Paint and tape, brushes and tarps."

Annalee rose and went into the kitchen to find Rusty and Andy at the table, talking about the rebuilding of Rusty's cabin, all the materials they'd need and the order of things to do.

They slept at Andy's that night. The cabin was uninhabitable, even dangerous without heat or electricity. Then they spent the morning and early afternoon on their hands and knees in the remains of Rusty's living room plucking, sifting, picking and sometimes tweezing pieces of walrus skull until every shard they could find had been placed in a box. When they were finished they stood looking down at it. Beside Annalee, leaning heavily against her leg and gazing up at her with affection, Bear panted wetly. She absently petted his shaggy head. The smell of smoke in her nostrils was pungent and all three humans and the dog were covered with a fine layer of soot and dust.

The tusks, although intact, would be the most difficult aspect of the rebuilding challenge, Andy said. He could reassemble the skull like a jigsaw puzzle but the tusks had received a liberal basting from pyromaniac Susan's nail polish bottle. Andy was flummoxed. He had never encountered a problem like this. His father could have solved it. Or his granddaddy, the greatest taxidermist of all time. But how?

"Nail polish," Andy mused. "And bright red. It seeped down in between those fine cracks in the ivory. What sort of stuff is like nail polish, Rusty?"

"Yeah, like I'd know the answer to that." He plucked a sliver of bone from his boots and placed it gently in the box. "I do my nails every day after I set my hair."

"Gotcha. Annalee? Do you use it?"

"I don't, but the hardware store where I work has a whole aisle devoted to solvents and I think that's what you need. If you can wait a few days until I get back, I'll go over the stock until I find something that will get the color out without harming the ivory. Acetone's the logical choice but it might stain and dry out the bone." She noticed that Rusty's expression had hardened.

"Well," Andy said, "I guess that's it. You guys come on back tonight. You ain't gonna stay here." Rusty nodded and they shook hands all around. Andy hoisted the box with one hand, seized Bear's collar with the other and thudded out to his truck.

Annalee and Rusty watched Andy's truck until it had disappeared and then continued to stare out toward the birches bending under their weight of snow. Annalee was not ready to turn and face the damage. And without Andy's reassuring banter and Bear's warm bulk against her leg, her awareness of Rusty was heightened. She wanted some disclosure from him. Now he took her hand and led her to the charred dining room table where one chair remained. He sat and pulled her onto his lap.

"So you're leaving. I know, no promises. But then what?"

"Rusty, I feel as if I'm split in two. Leaving my home, my friends, everything I know will be so hard. But here, this, this thing I feel here...."

"Do I have any part in this? I keep getting the feeling of just being your personal motel so you can get to this, this, this...." Rusty parodied Annalee but she understood his frustration.

"I care about you, of course I do. But Rusty, I still don't completely trust you. I have to be honest with you. I stayed alone for five years because Brad was unfaithful and I felt I could never trust again. It was such a shock. To go from that kind of isolation to pulling up my roots and going three thousand miles into the unknown to be with someone new? It's too hard for me. Give me six months."

"Six *months*? That's a long time, Annalee. Christ, that's half a year. What's going to happen down there in six months that can't happen here?"

"I have obligations. I have roots and ties. I need to find a way to say goodbye to everyone I know. And I need to get to know you better long-distance if I'm ever going to be with you. We'll talk every day if you want. I'll get a separate phone line just for you and me. I'll do whatever you want. You can come to California."

"No way. I'll be jealous of everything you see and touch."

"Don't be. You can trust me but I'll always be independent. You can't own me."

They remained there silently in the burned kitchen, in the hazy light with the sun casting shadows through axed slices in the walls, a cold breeze entering from the opening where a window had been, and flurries that heralded a new snowfall sifting across their shoulders. Neither moved even as the shadow of a moose nibbling bark fell across the charred wall.

"Rusty? There's something I need to know."

"Yeah, baby. Ask me anything."

"Where did you go when I was at Andy's?"

"Oh, that. I went to see a guy named Lenny."

"Please tell me he's not a hit man and you had him do something to Susan."

"No, he's a repo man and I had him do something to the red Camaro. Namely, repo it. Susan's car threw a rod right after she got here. That can happen when you try to drive a Wolfe tanning bed up the Al-Can Highway in a four-cylinder pickup. She thought she could show up here with no money so I gave her a loan for that piece of crap Camaro." He sighed. "That's eighty bucks I'll never see again. Come on. Let's head back to Andy's. I don't feel like working any more. In the morning we'll find whatever we can of yours that's not burned or wet or smoky. I need to get you to the airport by noon. I guess."

Chapter 18

Who Shall Be The First To Know

From her window seat Annalee could see Rusty on the tarmac at the pocket-sized Fairbanks airport, watching as her plane taxied out onto the runway. She cleared her mind and sat in silence as the engines revved, the speed increased and the small jet lifted aloft. As the landing gear lifted and stowed Annalee began to craft the news she would deliver to her loved ones and coworkers. And to brace for the inevitable response.

She had never played a part in the governance of the town, no politics or social machinations. But she knew her place. The locals recognized and depended upon her. There she was at her H.A.G.L. counter each day, The Princess Of Complaints, calmly exchanging one irrigation nozzle for another, soothing the tempers of dairy farmers when their pumps malfunctioned, offering exactly the right fencing supplies when those castaways from the upscale lifestyles of Southern California found their ostriches featured on the morning news, wandering on the freeway.

She would be leaving them now. How would she tell them, and when, and what to say?

From Fairbanks to Anchorage she wrote and rewrote the dramas in her mind, the news that she was moving to Alaska and the potential reactions that could range from outrage to disbelief to envy. During the two-hour layover in Anchorage she refined the scenes in her imagination. For the long journey from Anchorage down the coast of Canada she questioned herself, reassured herself, and solidified her commitment. Eventually, grainy-eyed and exhausted, she was finished.

The decision of whom to tell first was critical. Her parents, the most beloved, would be the last to know. There would be shock, tears, pleas, manipulation. Like the bare spotlight of an F.B.I. investigation their questioning would highlight any residual doubt or hesitation. So first, cowardly or not, she wanted to rehearse with others and bolster herself with whatever support she could find. That would mean relegating Ivy to the bottom of the list as well. Annalee winced as she considered the repercussions. Ivy. Her confidante, her best friend, the person who had put this cataclysm into motion. Ivy was already wounded by Annalee's secrecy. This news could permanently rend the delicate fabric of their relationship. Her colleagues at H.A.G.L.? Annalee played out the time line. She would tell T'Angeline, casually, out on the loading dock. She would swear T'Angeline to secrecy. And then ten minutes might elapse before T'Angeline would have pulled Ivy into the staff lounge to spill all. Oh my God, oh my God, Annalee is moving to Alaska to be with that guy in the sheepskin jacket! Why did Ivy not tell T'Angeline? Ivy did not know? Well, gosh, T'Angeline knew.... No, obviously Annalee could not confide in her colleagues. But who would be first? Her self-imposed isolation after Brad's rejection had resulted in a nearly hermetic social life.

    At Sea-Tac in Seattle Annalee stirred sugar into her coffee and squinted against the overhead fluorescent glare. The airport was nearly silent at 2 a.m. Outside in the fog the Alaska Airlines jet was loading passengers' luggage. A half hour remained before boarding time for San Francisco. Annalee felt suspended between opposing lifestyles. Behind her, Alaska seemed like a silent presence that waited, daring her to waiver and withdraw. Before her, San Amaro held the daunting challenge of disentangling herself from decades of history, alliances and familiarity. To whom could she turn for support and response?

    When she realized the answer it was as if she had always known. The litmus test would be the most emotionally sensitive, yet the most tough and daring woman she knew. Her sister. Evelyn, who knew drama, would be understanding and supportive. And of greatest importance would keep Annalee's plans a secret from their parents until the time was right. But Annalee wanted to look into her sister's eyes, watch her expression when she revealed the shocking news. She could easily change her schedule to include a hasty round trip to New Mexico, see Evelyn and be back in San Amaro by evening as planned.

A weary-sounding Alaska Airlines employee announced that all seats, all rows, anyone who was remotely interested in flying out of the penetrating darkness from Seattle to San Francisco could now board Flight 2460 for all she cared. Annalee took her seat. From there in a few hours she would see the sun rise over the San Francisco Bay.

⁓

Annalee felt as if her emotional state must be written on her face but no one seemed to notice her as she deplaned at San Francisco International, through the same doorway from which she had left, ten days yet a lifetime ago. It was the nature of airports, Annalee reflected. Each passenger seemed to have a story. A business woman in a severe tailored suit reading the paper in the coffee line. A young mother and twin boys, intertwined with parcels of diapers and formula and toys and the other baggage typical of travel with children. And the more exotic travelers, their appearance conjuring some assignation or escape or fantasy. Young men, pierced and tattooed. Heavily made up women. A man weeping as he picked over a rosary. Annalee gazed up at the overhead list of departures and arrivals. A flight would leave for Albuquerque in three hours. Annalee would telephone her sister when she arrived there at 9 a.m., she decided. There would be no reason to wake her now. This wasn't an emergency and there was no telling when Evelyn got out of bed these days, if she had slept.

Chapter 19

Evelyn Knows All

The desert sun was painting the surrounding hills with tawny amber, beige and sienna when Annalee phoned her sister from the Albuquerque airport. Evelyn said she was just rinsing out the coffee pot after her second cup and could pick her up in 20 minutes. Cliff had left for a tow truck call some 30 miles away and she had nothing to do until noon when she would start her rounds as a cleaning lady. She was surprised to hear that Annalee was in town but seemed less intrigued by her sister's aberrant behavior than Annalee expected. She didn't ask what Annalee was doing so far from home.

"I'd offer you a shot of brandy in your coffee," Evelyn said, "but there's no alcohol in this house any more. You look like you could use some liquid courage. Here. We'll put a shot of Taos honey in it." She dropped a dollop of the amber substance into Annalee's coffee and slid the cup across the table where Annalee sat with her unfocused gaze directed to an American flag affixed to the wall with thumbtacks. "Try your coffee," she prompted.

Annalee did a double-take at the cup and nodded abstractly. For the past half hour since arriving at Evelyn and Cliff's hardscrabble tract house on the outskirts of town she had mentally rehearsed her speech. She would approach carefully. She would reveal that she had been in Alaska, with a man. Once Evelyn had absorbed that news, hopefully without spiraling into an emotional overreaction, Annalee would fill in the gaps.

She noticed that her sister was now resting her chin on her hands and smiling with closed lips. She felt an ancient residual irritation.

Evelyn would affect this Cheshire posture and expression as a teenager when she was bursting with an annoying secret... for instance, that her sophomore science class had witnessed Annalee backing the family Chevrolet into a light pole. She set aside her discomfort and returned to refining her opening lines. Everything hinged on her first careful words and their delivery. She would strike a lighthearted tone. Guess where I've been, she would say. No, obviously not. She must be serious. Evelyn, she would say, I've been lonely but now... No, that would focus on Rusty. Evelyn, have you ever been drawn to Alaska? No, that would never....

Evelyn interrupted the silent monologue. "So," she said. "I hear you met some bush pilot named Rusty and ran off to Alaska."

Annalee was silent for an incredulous heartbeat as the room seemed to tilt. She grasped the edge of the table. And then she screamed.

Evelyn looked startled. "Jesus, Annalee, why the emotional overreaction?"

"Oh my God, oh my God, how did you guess?"

"I didn't guess. You left a trail a mile wide."

"*What?*"

"Well, first Mom called because you left a weird message about taking a little vacation in Alaska like you do it all the time. So I called Ivy. And she started babbling about some guy in a sheepskin jacket who showed up last winter and you started acting stoned. And now you're obsessed with Sheepskin Man and Ivy is sorry she ever gave you that damned Alaska bachelor magazine for Christmas." Annalee gasped. "She sounded upset and I didn't want to make it worse by asking too many questions. So I went down to the library. I asked, what magazine has something to do with bachelors in Alaska? Well! Apparently *Alaskan Bachelors* is the hottest thing to hit the singles scene since condoms. I nearly shit. Our Annalee is finally rejoining the living. Granted, shacking up with Eskimos is a strange way to do it but still, it's progress. Anyway, the library had all the back issues including the one from Christmas and after I read it I called Ivy again. I said, 'just curious, that guy in the sheepskin jacket. Was he skinny with red eyes?' She said no. 'Did he have a thick neck?' Uh-uh. 'Was he three feet tall with a barrel chest?'

No. 'Did he look like a slender young Steve McQueen but with shaggy blonde hair?' She said, 'yup.' So I figured Russell Lee, 'or Rusty to his friends' is Sheepskin Man. I can hardly wait to hear the story."

"I can't believe this. I absolutely cannot believe this. Did you tell anyone?" Annalee's breath was shallow and high in her chest.

"Annalee, you're 41 years old. You remind me of that Tanya Tucker song from the seventies, what was it called? Delta Dawn, that's it. You know . . . 'She's forty-one and her daddy still calls her baby . . . .' And Dad does still call you baby. Well, once in awhile he does and . . ."

"Focus, Evelyn! Did you tell Mom and Dad?"

"Sure. Why wouldn't I?"

"Oh no! How is Mom taking it? Is she coming to San Amaro? Is Dad really upset? Damn it, Evelyn, how could you? You know what they're like!"

"Yes, Annalee. I know what they're like. After I stopped using, it took about a month for the fog to lift from my brain but once I got clean and sober I knew they're actually perfectly ordinary parents. Pretty good ones, at that."

"I could just kill you! It was so important that they not find out until . . ."

Evelyn placed a palm on her sister's wrist and gently closed her fingers. "Annalee?"

"What!"

"Shut up."

Annalee fell silent, breathing heavily.

"I'll bet your coffee is cold. You're a waste of good Taos honey. Come with me." Evelyn stood and left the room.

Annalee, still fuming, followed her sister through the back door to an expanse of desert. The sun was reaching its zenith. Annalee saw in the distance the rounded peaks of the Sandias and, closer, saguaro cactus raising their arms to the sun. The acrid air and scent of desert sage, the dust in her nostrils were in sharp, uncomfortable contrast to the ambience of the Alaskan interior she had left only yesterday. The disparity made her long for that presence, the cold that bit yet nurtured, the sense of needing to meet a challenge that was just out of reach. Evelyn continued to walk toward the hills. Their heels crunched on the desert sand. No sounds broke the silence. Even the birds were quiet, seeking shade in the bright autumn sun.

"Remember when we were kids," Evelyn said eventually. Her voice was quiet, reflective. "And we would play hide and seek?"

"Yeah. In San Francisco. So what."

"And I used to think if I closed my eyes I'd be invisible and you couldn't find me?"

In spite of her outrage Annalee smiled as she remembered the child her sister had been, in pigtails and a leotard at age four with her eyes tightly shut, in plain view behind the family car, believing she could not be seen. Then Annalee realized where the reflection was leading. "I don't do that! I don't shut my eyes and think I'm invisible."

"I'm afraid you do. Do you think we've all been blind to you, Annalee? Like, if you shut your eyes we wouldn't see how badly you've been hurt? We know you miss love. We know how much Brad wounded you, you don't want to go through it again. But you want to try anyway. And finally you stopped lying to yourself and you did try. And maybe this new guy will hurt you too. But this is part of life. Open your eyes, Annalee. You're not invisible."

Chapter 20

Oh Tragedy

For the next four months Annalee pieced her way through the challenges of letting go. She took notes at work for her successor to use and looked at her landscape through new eyes. Each familiar sight brought an awareness of impending finality. Some day she would see this scene, that face, carry out this chore or habit for the last time. Everyone knew of her plan to leave for Alaska. Although she hadn't physically started to pack she had made lists of things to take, give away and discard. Cooper and Rachel, once recuperated from their initial astonishment and distress, agreed to return to San Amaro to move their antiques and finery into storage and prepare the house to rent.

Annalee tried, finally, to tell Ivy everything but it was Ivy herself who stifled those confidences.

"Ivy, if you could only see and feel what I did in Alaska you would..."

"Let me stop you right there. You're still my friend and I still love you but I'm still hurt. Maybe I'm wrong, maybe I'm selfish and egotistical, but for almost a whole year you cut me out of the most important thing that's happened since Brad left and right now I don't want your leftovers. I know you're leaving and why. That's enough. Besides, you're obviously doing just fine without me."

"But I'm not doing fine. I'm confused and overwhelmed one minute and then next minute I'm..."

"Hey. What part of 'I don't want to hear about it' don't you understand? Now, have some of these peanut butter cookies, guaranteed to take up permanent residence on your thighs."

As she promised, Annalee installed a separate telephone line for Rusty. With his cabin's repair on hold until summer, there was no phone service. Instead, every Saturday night he called from the general store/post office in Garnet.

"Can you believe it's been a year since our first phone conversation, Rusty?"

"I'm still shaking in my boots about our first phone conversation. Valentine's Day will always remind me never to tease a lady about her butt."

Annalee quelled a temptation to ask if there were still opportunities to tease women who filled his mailbox with innocently, or deliberately, provocative images.

"Annalee, can't I talk you into staying with me at least for the first few weeks? I know you're independent and all that. But compared to being here, San Amaro might as well be New York."

"No, Rusty, not yet. Maybe I'm unrealistic, and if I get in over my head I know I can count on you. But it's not about frozen water pipes and chopping wood. I'll be totally dependent on you for that and I hope you'll be patient. I need to be able to trust you in a relationship and it's too soon to start out living together."

"I hope you know what you're getting yourself into."

No matter what Annalee was doing, at 6 p.m. each Saturday she was in her father's study awaiting Rusty's call. And for the next four months it rang precisely on time.

And then, silence.

On the Saturday after the last of the Yukon River ice had flowed out to sea and Alaska had officially re-emerged from the frozen grip of winter, Rusty didn't call.

After one week Annalee was quizzical.

After two weeks she was angry.

By the third week she was panic-stricken. She couldn't bring herself to look up Andy's number or call the store in Garnet to ask the postmistress/cashier if anyone had seen Rusty. If he'd been lying to her after all she would feel like a stalker, like Susan, if her searching for him reached his ears.

After three weeks and four days, on a Tuesday evening the phone rang. Long after that night, when she could finally think clearly again, Annalee would repeat the conversation over and over in her mind.

"Are you . . . are you Annalee?" The woman's voice was unfamiliar.

"Yes, who's calling?"

"I'm sorry. I need to give you bad news."

"Oh dear. Is it my father?" In the back of her mind Annalee registered and denied the distant hiss of a call from Alaska.

"I found your phone number and some of your letters with Rusty's things. You need to know. Rusty's plane went down in the river three weeks ago."

"What? Oh my God. Is he OK?"

"No. He died on impact."

Before Annalee could respond the line went dead.

Horrified, she stared at the telephone as if it might yield further information. Or retract it. The room spun. Moments passed. And then with shaking fingers Annalee called her sister.

With Evelyn on one extension and Cliff on the other they tried to make sense of the news.

"Listen, Annalee," Cliff said. "This chick who called, do you think she could have just been fucking with you? From what you've said he don't have a history of latching on to stable women. Other than you."

"I don't know. I can't think. How would I find out?"

"Do you know his parents?" Evelyn asked.

"Do you know the number on the tail of his airplane?" This from Cliff.

"Parents, no. But tail number, yes." She went for his *Alaskan Bachelors* profile which she kept with other treasured artifacts in her vanity table. "What now, Cliff?"

"One of my buddies is a 'Nam vet and he flew copters. He still flies as a hobby. He'd know how to trace that number through the National Transportation Safety Board. If the plane went down they'd know, especially if there was a fatality."

Two hours later they called back and it was Evelyn who gave her the news.

"Annalee, I'm so terribly sorry and I'll come to San Amaro right away if you want. The report says Blue Lady spiraled left for an unknown reason and then pancaked into the Yukon upside-down. It crashed through two feet of ice. They reported it as one of the worst crashes in the past ten years. And Annalee, I don't want to tell you this but there were two passengers. The pilot, Russell Lee. And a female passenger identified as Kathleen Macomb. They both died."

With some deeply-buried awareness Annalee knew that when she emerged from shock she would not be the same. Not as a daughter, friend, sister, coworker, neighbor, or some day in the vast distant future a lover. She needed to prepare a nest for her grief.

Evelyn promised to call their parents and Ivy and Marvin.

"What can I tell them?"

"Tell them everything. I haven't kept secrets any more but Ivy didn't want the details. You'll need to fill her in. Tell them I need some time to be alone. And then, I don't know."

"Cliff and I can be there on the next flight west, Annalee. Just say the word."

While she could still function, in the brief grip of that adrenalin which precedes shock Annalee took stock of her kitchen, raced to the store for vitamins, green vegetables and fruit, comfort food and nutrition. Her stomach had already begun to churn so she shopped quickly, ran back to her car, fled home and then put all three bags in the refrigerator—cans of soup, toothpaste and all.

The next few days passed in a fog. Sometimes Annalee would pace the floor, hold a pillow to her chest, plead with a nameless deity to give her direction or reason. "What do you want, what do you want from me, what should I do," she would cry. Sometimes at night she would go out onto the deck, the place where she would so often talk to Rusty, and look up at the sky. It seemed vast, larger and deeper and more silent than ever before. She watched mindless sitcoms on television and then grief would smite her like an ocean wave and she would fall to the floor.

After the first week the haze lifted and her raw emotions would yaw from dissociation to penetrating sorrow. The sense of unreality seemed like madness and slipped its fingers into every corner of her life. Who was Kathleen, the woman who died with Rusty? Had everything about Rusty been fabricated? In fact, was Ivy who she said she was? Marvin? Did T'Angeline lead a secret life? Her own reflection passing the window would startle her and her heart would crash in her chest. She would forget to eat until she was dizzy. In her lucid moments she would call her sister.

"I can't get my mind around it, Evelyn. I start running these scenarios. It was a different plane, they made a mistake, the woman with him was his elderly neighbor."

"Annalee, denial isn't always bad. It gives you a break from your feelings. Not everything they say at Narcotics Anonymous meetings is crap. But denial can get pretty twisted, so just try to keep one foot planted in reality."

"Are you talking to Mom and Dad?"

"I told them everything and that you would talk to them when you're able to but right now you needed to be alone."

"Evelyn, I'm so grateful to you. And to the folks for respecting my needs. I'll bet Mom is pacing by the phone, wanting to call but keeping her word. And Dad. If I ask he'd be here in a minute."

"Why don't you ask, then?"

"I'm afraid they'd smother me."

"Maybe people aren't always the way you think they are."

"That's an understatement."

⁓

Each episode of grief in life brings with it, like a contrail, the residue of all grief that came before. Annalee had work to do. She had always thought herself lucky. No one in her family other than ancient aunts and uncles had died. No friends had been brought down by accident or disease. She had been among the fortunate ones to achieve middle age without mourning. That fantasy yielded to reality as Annalee finally allowed herself to move through loss. She had never grieved the two miscarriages or the end of her marriage, but the grief was there awaiting her. Even with the tragedy of Rusty demanding her attention, her irrational guilt over the miscarriages and her anger over the betrayal of Brad finally surfaced. Complex grief laid a patina over everything.

Soon she came to visualize herself as the survivor of a devastating railway accident. At first her wounds were raw and bleeding, and then messy scabs formed. They seeped and suppurated but she was whole. Three weeks into her mourning Annalee left the house for the first time. She went to the gym and pounded the treadmill until her face streamed with sweat. When she went home she thought she saw a glimmer of healing on the horizon, and then the grief descended again and knocked her to her knees.

It went on that way for days.

And then the spans of immobilizing sorrow and frantic confusion was interleaved with some ancient knowledge of life and its mystery. The pain shortened and sanity lengthened. She could not bear any thought or sign of Alaska or airplanes and the sight of snow in a news report about a blizzard back east plummeted her back into immobilizing depression. But she was able to sleep and, almost, to eat normally. Her interest in food had vanished but she deliberately added protein and a range of vitamins to her salads, often her only meal of the day.

Six weeks after the news, Annalee returned to H.A.G.L. and realized it was too soon. Like someone who is too optimistic after invasive surgery she spent an hour behind her counter and then sped home. That day, without feeling the transition, Annalee's sorrow fractured and rage rushed in.

Few objects at Annalee's house were safe. Sometimes she would stand in the back yard and slam ceramic flower pots to the concrete walkway to hear the crash and see the shards. When she couldn't throw with enough force she stood on the picnic table for additional height. She stopped short of decimating her mother's Spode and Waterford. She broke only what was hers.

She metaphorically threw a flower pot at her high school psychology professor. Fuck you and your stages of grief, she cried. Denial, anger, bargaining, depression and, oh, right, acceptance, who the fuck makes up this crap? She slammed another flower pot to the deck. She wasn't about to bargain with anyone for anything. Life had been one cruel joke after another. She threw a dish, kicked the shards and then threw the shards at the fence and screamed. She hoped her neighbors wouldn't call 911.

The caller who had delivered the news of Rusty's death—who was that woman? In her madness Annalee discounted his ex-wife, his many daughters and sisters. The woman who went down into the water with Rusty was one of his lovers and the caller was another in a hideous cosmic prank, another she-devil smiting Annalee through the telephone. Annalee felt a warped need to inflict the pain she felt and spun scenarios of appearing in Garnet to reveal her identity to the grieving caller. She discarded each fantasy simply because of the physical obstacles. And if she had carried out her drama she would relinquish Rusty forever. In some grief-deranged spot in her psyche, if she didn't physically confront a person or place, Rusty wasn't dead.

Week after week she bounced from depression to anger to wisdom to a weary sickness over the consuming chore of mourning.

Chapter 21

The Odds Are Good But the Goods Are Odd

A month passed. Annalee went to H.A.G.L. each day but was vacant-eyed and often left early. Her air of frailty prompted colleagues and customers to lower their voices in her presence. At noon she sat out on the loading dock and looked into the hills with her unopened lunch bag at her side. Twice Ivy came out to keep her company but found her friend unresponsive. They sat in silence until Ivy sighed and returned to the staff lounge to eat alone.

And then, on a Sunday evening, Annalee's doorbell rang. She opened to see Ivy on the doorstep in her usual H.A.G.L. uniform: spiked hair gelled to points around her tiara, work boots, Levi's belted low at her hips and a denim shirt. With Ivy were Sheila of Drapery Cove, T'Angeline, Oscar The Overlord of Nuts And Bolts. There was her boss Marvin Phee and his son Marvin Phee Junior. And Marvin Phee Junior's son, Marvin Phee Junior Junior or JJ. The unexpected visitors held wine bottles and brown paper bags. An aroma of garlic, lemon, herbs, chicken, broth and seafood wafted into the foyer.

"Uh... hi?" Annalee said.

"We are here," Ivy intoned, "because we miss you and need you back. If you're going to act like a baby we're going to treat you like one. We are going to feed you and then we are going to change you. Anyway, we're going to change your mood."

She elbowed her way past Annalee, trailed by her cohorts. As Annalee watched, amazed, the crowd moved around the dining area, rummaging in cabinets and cupboards. Oscar found a damask tablecloth and flung it onto the dining table. JJ selected plates, bowls and flatware from the china cabinet while his grandfather Marvin opened bottles of Chardonnay. On the kitchen counter top, Ivy arranged the take-out cartons and T'Angeline began to set the table. Over her shoulder she called, "I just can't wait any more! Sheila made something for you, Annalee. Show her, Sheila!"

Sheila reached into a cavernous handbag and withdrew a long scarlet sheath dress with a plunging neckline. It shimmered like water as she held it up.

T'Angeline gushed, "Sheila sews these silk things for pornography stores!"

"I do not!"

"Anyway, you can't buy one unless you can prove you're single."

"T'Angeline, be quiet. Annalee, I learned how to sew with silk last year and just for fun I started making these garments. They're simple but they really took off. Now I have them in . . . ."

"She sells them all over the place, Annalee! San Francisco, Sausalito, and she has an ad in cosmetic surgery places in Hollywood for a discount if you get your boobs done."

"T'Angeline, put something in your mouth. Like I was going to say, I supply only to upscale boutiques. And yes, I do have a consignment with Chatterley." Sheila glared at T'Angeline who, apparently oblivious to the tone, smiled happily around an egg roll she was eating with her fingers. Annalee knew Chatterley as an adult toy and movie store on the far side of town.

"But they sell more than dildos and cherry vanilla condoms in there. They sell tasteful, elegant apparel for the boudoir." Sheila sounded as if she were reciting from a catalogue. "Anyway, we were trying to think of a gift and your mom told Ivy you might have liked that yellow blouse they gave you even though you took it off as soon as they weren't looking. So we decided you might like this. We hope you feel better."

Annalee was genuinely touched. "Thank you, Sheila and everyone. It really is gorgeous."

"Ok, you guys. Sit," Ivy barked. She guided Annalee to the head of the table. "We are here because we love Annalee." There was a small round of applause. "And we want her to be feeling better. So Annalee, we wish to present you with this feast of won ton soup, egg rolls, Kung Pau chicken, sweet and sour pork, beef with something-or-other, garlic shrimp, and one fortune cookie apiece from Happy Noodle Garden.

We're all going to enjoy it so if you insist on maintaining your hunger strike fuck you and we'll eat it ourselves."

"Hear, hear." This from Marvin.

"And we would like you to wear your red dress right now as a symbol of your agreement that you're feeling better, even if you're not, because we're ready to kill you." There was more applause.

Feeling an old sense of glee and fun, so far in the past that they seemed nearly unique, Annalee stood and slipped the garment over her head. She allowed the material to ripple down over the sweat suit she had worn for two days. "My God, this is so beautiful. Thank you so much! Wait. I'm going to get one of Mom's aprons. I'll never forgive myself if I get Kung Pau on this dress."

"That's more like it," Ivy crowed. "Obsessive and compulsive, just the way we like her."

Marvin poured wine into the Waterford crystal. "You're not supposed to have Chardonnay with beef," he said, "but we're family, not tourists. A toast to Annalee!"

For the next hour they passed around the cartons, ate and drank and chatted about work, weather and the potential for that year's grape harvest. They teased and told stories about the customers and all their projects and problems. No one pressured Annalee to join in, but when she did they simply included her. It was like old times. Annalee felt the start of a new commitment to change. These friends who loved her deserved more than the withdrawn wraith she had been for so long.

Finally, after the dishes were cleared and the fortune cookies read aloud, Marvin opened a bottle of dessert wine and poured a helping for each guest.

Ivy said, "And now, Annalee, we have work to do." Silence filled the dining room as her coworkers turned to face Annalee. "We want you to think of some way to change your environment, to symbolically take control. Of this house, if nothing else. It's a start. You grew up here. You returned here in pain. And now we want to change this place for you so that you can continue to be here but in peace, in harmony, in the love of your friends and family. Change something, Annalee. Something big. What will it be? Paint? Carpets? Want us to bring in chain saws and hack a skylight in the kitchen ceiling? Whatever it is, we'll do it."

Annalee needed little time to reflect. "Actually, yes, you guys. I've always wanted a way to control the lighting in here. Dim and raise it, set different moods."

"Different moods, just the thing," everyone murmured their approval.

Marvin Junior slapped a hand on the dining room table. "Rheostat!" he cried. He tossed his car keys to JJ. "To H.A.G.L. with you, son. You know where to find them."

JJ sprinted from the room. Soon he returned, breathless, with a H.A.G.L. bag. "They had about 87 different rheostats," he said. "I got one of each."

Familiar with the stock, Annalee knew that H.A.G.L. offered 15 rheostats. Some attached to lamps, some went outside, some inside, and one deluxe model featured a dial to control the precise mood in each room, from dim to blazing. This was Annalee's choice. The installation required the party to turn off all electrical power. With Annalee's home plunged into blackness, Marvin, JJ and Oscar removed the light switch panels in each room and managed the hardware while the others held flashlights, opened bubble packs and facilitated the installation.

When they were finished they followed Annalee throughout her home, cheering and applauding each time she changed the darkness to light.

༄

Some areas of Annalee's life still felt raw. She still could not allow mention of Alaska, and the sight of a small airplane overhead would catapult her into another episode of weeping. But she went to work each day and was present for the customers and her coworkers. She ate, she slept, and she kept true to her promise to her friends. Each day she wore some article of color. The red dress was on a hanger and set aside for special occasions but she wore an orange belt one day, a royal blue barrette in her hair the next to bring out the blue in her eyes, a black blouse with yellow buttons and yellow socks to match. She could not see far enough into the future to plan any change other than what to wear and what to eat the next day but she was functioning.

And she was haunted by a conflict. She felt a persistent, nagging need to know the whole story of the crash in tandem with an equally intense desire to avoid the disturbing details. The terse report from the N.T.S.B. didn't tell her what had caused Blue Lady to plummet from the sky, it didn't identify the passenger with Rusty, and of course it didn't detail the horror and confusion that must have been felt by witnesses. She knew one person in Garnet who could tell the story and finally, in a quiet moment in the garden on a Sunday morning in May, she was ready to hear it.

As she heard the phone ring in Andy's cabin she smiled to recall the woman she had been, shakily approaching the stairwell in his house as he proudly led her to a basement she imagined would be filled with dismembered parts and buckets of blood.

"Do I remember you? For heaven's sake, Annalee, how could I forget? I've been worried about you. How have you been?"

"It's been a hard six months, Andy."

"I wanted to call you when it happened but I didn't know your last name or where you lived in California. Then I heard Mary Beth found your number and she told you. We still haven't got over it. It was a nightmare. I hope you had a lot of family and friends to take care of you down there."

"I did. I do. But there are some questions, Andy, and I hope you can help. My sister got the report from the Safety Board but it didn't give the whole story. Andy, what happened to Blue Lady? And who was Kathleen, the woman with Rusty when the plane went down?"

"It was Katie, Annalee. You must have met her. That girl who was always following Rusty's brother around? Rusty and Kenny wanted to try out some new pontoons on the floatplane and Katie wasn't going to let Kenny out of her sight so she had to go too. Rusty was never good at saying no to a woman. He took a dangerous chance and paid dearly. There were three people in a plane that was meant for two. Katie and Kenny both went down with Rusty. That report must have been the preliminary. Kenny was ... He was ejected when the plane hit the water and since they only found two bodies they thought at first there were only two passengers. They found Kenny's remains on the riverbank later but it took weeks for the coroner's report to positively identify him.

So Katherine was poor deluded, obsessive Katie.

"Their families must be devastated," Annalee said. "Katie's and, God knows, Kenny and Rusty's parents in Georgia. Losing both sons like that." They shared a silence. "I'd like to contact Rusty's family to express my condolences. The woman who called me, you said her name is Mary Beth? Was that one of his sisters or daughters? He had a bunch of each. She didn't say who she was. After she told me what happened, she just hung up. It was strange but I guess she was too upset to talk. Do you have her number?"

"Ah...."

In his hesitance Annalee sensed what was coming. And somehow, like a miracle, the news carried no weight. She simply felt sadness, acceptance and, at last, letting go.

"Mary Beth wasn't family, Annalee. I didn't like the idea of her being the one to call you but by the time I found out, she'd already talked to you and there was nothing I could do. Rusty never really believed you were coming back and Mary Beth was always hanging around. She was just one of these women who moved up here to find a husband. I guess she didn't mind the thing they always say about single men in Alaska." Annalee and Andy chorused the words together. "The odds are good, but the goods are odd."

Chapter 22

Familiar Sensations

Annalee reminded herself to breathe deeply and evenly. She reached up to push a wisp of hair from her eyes. At two weeks before her 43rd birthday there was a generous mix of silver with the auburn but it was unruly as always. She had tied it into a bun atop her head but tendrils would escape. She couldn't risk having her vision interrupted.

She briefly flexed her legs and then shifted in her seat, making certain that she was restrained but not impaired. She heard the slight jangle of metal on metal of the clasps and buckles at her shoulder, chest and across her hips.

"Now shut your eyes," the man beside her said. Annalee did as she was told. "Turn the key." She did so and felt the vibration that always thrilled and frightened her no matter how often she experienced it and how well she knew the source.

"Feel with your senses so that if there's anything strange or unfamiliar, you'll know and you'll stop." Annalee was aware of only familiar sensations. The vibration under her seat and around her, the rough aroma of aviation fuel. And the odor of fish carried on a moist puff of air that blew into her right ear. She smiled, opened her eyes and reached back to pat Bear who always claimed his seat in the holding area between the pilot and passenger in her Cessna.

"OK," Andy said from the copilot seat beside her. "You've completed all the reading and practicing, you've logged all the required hours. Your first time at the controls should be easy. Now take 'er up, Annalee."

About the Author

Marsh Rose is a psychotherapist, college educator and freelance writer. Her short stories have appeared in *Cosmopolitan Magazine, Salon.Com*, the *San Francisco Sunday Chronicle, Chronicle Datebook*, the *San Francisco Examiner, Redwood Coast Review*, "This I Believe" on NPR, and *Carve Magazine*. She lives in northern California.

CPSIA information can be obtained at www.ICGtesting.com
Printed in the USA
BVOW011325300113

311971BV00001B/11/P